TAIL
&
TROUBLE

VICTOR
CATANO

Tail and Trouble
A Red Adept Publishing Book

Red Adept Publishing, LLC
104 Bugenfield Court
Garner, NC 27529
http://RedAdeptPublishing.com/

Print ISBN-13: 978-1-940215-68-6
Print ISBN-10: 1-940215-68-4

First Print Edition: April 2016

Cover and Formatting: Streetlight Graphics

To Kim, for all the love, encouragement and inspiration.

*And to Ollie. Thank you for letting me into
the pack. You are always missed.*

ONE

I INCHED MY RED FORD GALAXIE forward. Orson lay in the passenger seat, splayed out, with his tongue lolling out of his mouth. He had dozed off as if he hadn't a care in the world. The barely there AC wheezed and whimpered, harmonizing with Orson's snoring.

The road to Charleston was clogged with midday commuters and early weekend traffic. Ahead were flashing emergency lights. We weren't going anywhere, and we had places to be. Annoyed, I started to drum my fingers on the wheel. That didn't last long, as the vinyl was so hot I was afraid my hand would get stuck to it.

The fan blew hot air in my face. I checked the temperature gauge. The arrow was creeping up to the red. I sighed. The last thing I needed was to overheat on the highway.

I tapped Orson on his furry brown leg. He opened his eyes and favored me with a disdainful stare.

I motioned to the traffic jam. "Little help?"

Orson yawned, scratched behind one ear with a back paw, then gave his privates a lick just to make sure they were still there. Finally, he glanced up at the road. He barked once, a spark flaring in his eyes.

The police lights went off as the accident got cleared over to the shoulder. The traffic began to move. As our speed got back above thirty, the engine cooled a bit.

Happy? Too hot. Let me sleep.

I felt the thought in my head, gruff and growling. It was

like an itch I couldn't scratch. I patted him on the head. "Thanks, Orson."

He grunted and was back asleep in under a minute. The way the bulldog's hindquarters were twitching, he was probably dreaming about violating an uptight poodle. I smiled. Orson had a way with the ladies, human and canine.

The thermometer was still too close to the red for my liking, so I decided to pull off the freeway to give the car a rest. The next exit was for Myrtle Beach. Sheila had always been a beach person. She loved to sit on the hot sand and watch the waves; I loved to see her in a swimsuit. When I flipped on my turn signal, Orson's eyes popped open, and he sat up in the seat. He whined pitifully. He liked beaches, too. And he missed his mama. We had been on the road for over eight hours, trying to find her trail.

We had to circle around for a minute, but we finally got a spot in an ideal location, close to both a hot dog stand and the beach. After Orson and I had walked along the shore line and splashed our feet in the bathtub-warm surf, I bought us lunch: a plain hot dog for Orson, chili cheese for me. Orson wanted chili, but I said no. Maybe if he didn't sleep with his butt in my face, I would reconsider. Orson wolfed his down in a minute. I leaned against the car and ate mine, the thirteen-year-old part of my brain snickering at a gift shop called the Gay Dolphin. I was sure there was an innocent reason for the name, but I couldn't help imagining a dolphin on rollerblades.

The groups of college kids gave us a wide berth. Even though there were plenty of No Dogs Allowed signs, no one bothered us. People didn't really notice Orson unless he wanted to be noticed.

And he definitely wanted those two blond sorority girls in bikinis to notice him. I mentally dubbed them Muffy and Buffy.

"Oooh, he's adorable!" Muffy squealed. "I love bulldogs!"

"Can I pet him?" Buffy cooed.

Orson was already rubbing his head against her leg, the gold flecks in his brown eyes flashing. Muffy and Buffy didn't wait for an answer. Both bikini-clad girls bent over and petted his back. Orson bobbed his head up, pressing it against their breasts.

"He's so funny!" Muffy said. "He thinks he's people!"

If you only knew.

Orson rolled onto his back, and the girls cooed as they rubbed his belly.

You dirty dog.

Orson grinned. *Don't hate the player.*

Two frat boys jogged up. Their build and their attitude told me they were probably football players. Since they were both under six feet and a little thick around the waist, I guessed they were small college, big enough to be irritating but small enough that they had to prove how tough they were every chance they got.

"Hey, what's going on?" one asked.

"What you doing with our ladies, brah?" the other one added.

Sigh. "I'm not doing anything, *brah.* Your ladies asked to pet my dog."

Orson twitched ecstatically as the two girls continued to scratch his belly.

The first one took a step closer. "Well, they can stop."

I gestured at the petting-fest. "No one's forcing them." That was mostly true. Orson couldn't force people to do anything completely against their will. But everybody wanted to pet Orson.

The second one waved at the girls. "Yo, Kylee, come on."

"Yeah, let's go, Buffy," the first one added.

Huh. Her name really was Buffy. The two girls ignored the guys and continued to coo over Orson, getting dangerously close to breaking whatever animal husbandry laws South Carolina might have had.

Chad and Biff moved closer to me and puffed out their chests, glaring.

"What the fuck, man?" Biff said.

"Yeah, what the fuck?" Chad echoed.

"Like I said, no one is forcing your ladies to pet my dog. If they would rather pet him than talk to you, can you blame them? Orson is a lot more charming than the two of you."

They furrowed their unibrows. After a second, their eyes popped wide. I thought I even heard them growl. I knew I shouldn't goad them. Sheila was always telling me I would insult the wrong person one day. Not that I was worried about a fight. The day I couldn't handle two stupid frat boys was the day they could put me in a home to eat lime Jell-O and watch *Law & Order* reruns. I wasn't huge and my army training hadn't given me bulging muscles, so a lot of idiots who were bigger than I was thought they could push me around. They didn't try that more than once.

Biff glared at me. "What did you say, brah?"

Oh well. In for a penny. I spread out against the hood of the car, my left hand resting near the antenna. I shifted my weight, so I'd be ready to move. "What, are you deaf *and* stupid?"

Chad's nostrils flared, and he lunged at me. I snapped off the antenna and whipped it at him. *Whap!* A cut opened up under his eye. He clapped a hand over the wound and fell back. Before Biff could react—*whap!*—he screamed and grabbed his face. Chad swung blindly at me. I sidestepped then gave him a straight palm to his nose. Blood flowed from his face, and he crumpled into a heap.

The two girls were still purring at Orson. Someone else would probably notice the bloodied frat boys, though. I picked up Orson and dumped him in the passenger seat. I slid in beside him and drove off.

Hey! We were having a moment! Go play with your friends some more.

I checked the rear view mirror. The girls were still bent over where Orson had been. They kind of shook themselves awake, then they noticed their boyfriends rolling around on the sidewalk. I could hear them scream from two blocks away.

TWO

WE GOT BACK ON THE highway and headed out of town. Once we were a safe distance away, I glared at Orson. "Well, you were no help at all back there."

Sorry. Too busy having fun. Try it sometime.

"Yeah. Well, your fun nearly got us in trouble."

Really? You took them in five seconds. What is trouble? Ten?

"Just because you can't resist a tummy rub."

Orson grinned, his tongue lolling dangerously far out of his mouth. *Maybe if I had a chili dog, I wouldn't have noticed them.*

"I should just get you neutered."

Orson growled, and I grinned. I would never do that to Orson. Sheila would kill me if I did anything to him, even something recommended by Bob Barker. Still, it helped to remind him that I could, especially when he tried to be too cute.

Sheila would never say that.

I frowned. "Sheila's not here."

Don't I know it.

It had been two weeks since we'd seen Sheila. Her coven had been asking her to do more and more for them, and she wasn't always comfortable with her assigned tasks. That had caused tension between us. I would tell her that she didn't have to do everything they wanted, especially if they were pressuring her, and she'd sigh and say it wasn't that easy. But there had been nothing to indicate that she would leave me, and even if the fights had gotten to that point, she would never have left without Orson.

Orson was her dog. That was how we met. Orson had been chasing after some piece of tail in the park. Sheila ran after him, her long dark hair whipping behind her, and she didn't see the handsome man stepping into her path until she ran into him. That handsome guy being me.

Three years later, Orson still wouldn't admit if he had arranged the meeting on purpose. He claimed that he had caught the scent of a Weimaraner, but I didn't remember seeing any other dogs in the park that day.

Orson also claimed not to know where Sheila was. The infuriating thing was that I believed him. They were linked. If Sheila wanted us to find her, Orson would know, provided she was still alive. I was certain Orson would feel it if she wasn't, and I was sure he would tell me. Well, pretty sure.

I opened the glove box and pulled out the Snausage bag. "Sorry, pal. That was too far."

Orson hoovered up the treats then chuffed. *Me too.*

"I miss her, you know."

Me too.

"Mmm-Mama." Orson whined and barked the words out loud.

Yes, Orson. Mama, indeed. I sighed and scratched that spot behind his ear. He rolled onto his back for more.

Turn on the radio.

"Shut up."

After another four hours in my hotbox of a car, we stopped at a 7-Eleven for radiator coolant. I picked up some taquitos for Orson. They weren't fit for human consumption, but Orson drooled with anticipation. No accounting for taste.

The sun was setting, making the night a little cooler.

I sat on the hood of the Galaxie, ate a Lunchable, and thought about Sheila.

She had been distracted and distant for a while. Something was obviously on her mind, but she wouldn't tell me what was going on. Orson wouldn't, either. There weren't two people closer than she and I, except maybe for her and Orson.

She had left the apartment to get the Sunday *New York Times*, and that was the last I had seen of her.

Orson and I scoured the streets around our New York apartment on the Upper West Side, then we drove from Battery Park up to Yonkers. We searched Riverside Park, the Cloisters, and the Sheep's Meadow, all of her favorite places, but she wasn't there. Usually, Orson could talk to her and sense her presence, but he couldn't get a bead on her. After two weeks with no word from her, we became desperate. So with reluctance, I checked in with her friends at the coven.

I had never really gotten along with the witches of Sheila's coven. I tolerated them because they were important to her, and they did the same for me, for the most part. When I entered the backroom of the New-Age bookstore where they held their meetings, I could feel the chill as twelve sets of eyes glared at me.

"She was destined for great things," Ramona said. The High Priestess shook her long black hair. "But she was getting distracted. She was putting other things ahead of the Order."

"I know you've never cared for me, but Sheila's missing. I haven't heard from her in two weeks."

"Just like a man." Maureen sniffed. "Always thinking it's about him." She had never liked me. Sheila had once taken me to a coven Solstice party, and Maureen got all huffy that a man had violated their circle.

"What are you worried about?" Ramona asked. "She's been away before."

Sheila did sometimes travel on business and "business." She sold supplies to new-age stores across the country, and she also hunted for esoterica and historical items for the coven. But she always left me a note. Sometimes, the messages were a sudden and a little vague, but they were always there. Once, she and Orson had disappeared after leaving behind only a Post-It that read "BRB: Off to Cheyenne!" I woke up a week later to find the two of them in bed next to me and a pair of incredible black boots on the floor. I wore those boots all the time after that.

"Yes, but not this long. Not without calling. Is she out on a job for you?"

Ramona smiled mockingly. "I can't say. I don't like to discuss our affairs with outsiders. Besides, if she is missing, how do we know you didn't do something to her?"

It took every ounce of willpower I had not to throttle her smug little neck. Orson barked.

Lisa looked down at him. She was Sheila's closest friend in the coven. When someone called a woman handsome, Lisa was the person they had in mind. She had a pleasant bearing and attitude, but her eyes had aged with worry lines.

"I've heard reports of witches being harassed all over the place," Ramona continued. "How do we know you aren't trying to cover your tracks by pretending to search for her?"

"Stop it!" Lisa yelled. "Do you think Orson would be with him if he did anything to Sheila?"

A murmur rose from the others.

I glared at them. "Please, if you know something, tell me. She's never been gone for so long without letting us know where she is."

No one responded. Lisa shifted her gaze between Ramona and me. She opened her mouth as if to say something then closed it. There was nothing left to do.

I walked out of the backroom and was at the back door when Lisa ran after me.

"Gabriel, wait!" She put her hand on my shoulder. "I'm sorry about Ramona."

"Can you help?" I asked in a rush, hoping that she would respond better separated from the rest of the witches. "Do you have any idea where Sheila might have gone? She'd been in a bad mood ever since she got back from the last trip she went on for you. What did she get?"

"It's hard to explain."

"Lisa, please. I'm begging you. It's been weeks. I'm desperate. Why would she leave without Orson? What could have happened?"

"I don't know. When she came back, she didn't have what we asked her to find. She wouldn't talk about it, either."

"Where did you send her?"

She hesitated. "I'm really not supposed to say. It was coven business."

I tried not to roll my eyes. The coven was worse than the mafia with their *omerta* bullshit. If it was "coven business," it was going to be shrouded in secrecy, even though it was probably something monumentally petty. Ramona could be extremely demanding and bossy, and Sheila sometimes got fed up with her.

Once Sheila had been sworn to secrecy about some coven business when she had to go out of state to find something. It turned out to be a case of Moxie soda for Ramona's birthday. When I asked her why that was such a big secret, Sheila said that the coven had powerful enemies, and if they knew what kind of drinks Ramona liked, anything could happen. She kept a straight face for three seconds then fell back on the bed, laughing, her gold-flecked hazel eyes twinkling.

I had chuckled with her. "Moxie tastes so bad, how could you tell if it was poisoned?"

THREE

A T NINE O'CLOCK, WE PULLED off the highway north of Jacksonville and found a cheap motel. After driving all day, I was exhausted. But I still spent a few hours staring at the water-stained ceiling until I passed into a fitful sleep with awful dreams. Dreams of Sheila being sucked into a black void. Dreams where I was holding her hand then suddenly not. Dreams where I could feel the terrifying ache of complete loneliness. Just before dawn, a noisy fart from Orson woke me up. *Damn taquitos.*

The motel wasn't the kind with a personal coffee maker or a free continental breakfast buffet. The office had a walk-up window made of inch-thick Plexiglas with a little slot for transactions. I loaded Orson in the car then shoved the key through the slot. The groggy-looking clerk only grunted.

We crossed Jacksonville and stopped at a McDonald's right outside of town. Orson loved fast food. It drove Sheila crazy. She had tried. She had bought him the best dog food, all natural, organic, and whole grain. She'd even made his food from scratch when the vet said he should improve his diet: a foul-smelling stew of liver, beef tongue, and brown rice that seemed to be always simmering on the stove. It didn't matter. Chubby little Orson had eaten a hamburger once, and that was it.

Once we'd made it through the drive-thru, Orson pawed at the wrapper and drooled on the seat in anticipation.

"You'd think for all the junk food I slipped you, you'd tell me where Sheila is."

Told you. Don't know. He whined pitifully.

"You've lied about this before."

That was different. She was trying to surprise you.

Sheila had been planning a birthday dinner for me and had gone to New Jersey to get my favorite chicken parmesan sub. So Orson had told me she was at the coven.

It wasn't the same situation. I knew that, but I was clinging to threads. "You're her familiar. Aren't you in contact with her all the time?"

Yes. But I can't hear anything. I can't help it. When Mama don't talk, I can't listen. She's not dead. Maybe she's shielding herself.

"Has she done that before?"

No.

Right out of high school, I had joined the Army to get money for college. That was what I told myself, anyway. I really joined to escape small-town rural poverty and a drunk father. Step one of the Army was shutting off your brain and accepting whatever bullshit they fed you. *You are going to serve your country!* Sure, okay. *There are WMDs in Iraq!* Whatever, hoss. *We will be welcomed as liberators!* Not even the dumbest grunts bought that one.

Even after being trained to believe anything I was told in the military, it was a stretch to believe some of the things Sheila told me. Magic protector dogs were the least of it. She lived in a world of charms, spells, and incantations. But I was far more willing to accept whatever she said while naked in bed.

"You're not listening," Sheila had said one night.

Sheila had a lovely birthmark under the swell of her right breast. If I looked at it right, it was like a pair of lips waiting for a kiss. Damn right I wasn't listening. "Sure I am."

"Then what did I just say?"

"That you would love for me to make you an omelet for breakfast right after I explore your body with my tongue."

She rolled her eyes. "Listen, or I put my shirt on."

I shifted my gaze upward, reluctantly.

"I know you think this is all crazy." When I started to protest, she put her finger on my lips. "I *know*. I can feel it. I'm sensitive like that." She pointed at her head. "Believe me, it was the same for me when it started."

"What do you mean? Can you tell what I'm thinking?"

"I can always tell what you're thinking. I don't need to be a mind reader for that." She kissed me. "Ever since I was a kid, I knew I was different. I knew when Mom and Dad were fibbing to me."

"Like about Santa Claus?"

"No, more like when they got divorced, and they were trying to hide it from me. They kept telling me everything was fine, but I knew it wasn't. I just *knew*."

"So you were intuitive. My mom kept telling me how everything was fine, even after Dad gave her a black eye. I could tell she was lying, too."

"Sure, but it was more intense than that. I could hear her voice in my head. *How will we get by? I know he's screwing that tramp at work.* It was so loud, like she was talking to me. I asked Mom what 'screwing' meant. She acted like I'd just slapped her."

"Spooky."

"Mom thought so. She was scared of me after that. I could tell. How can a mother be scared of an eight-year-old girl?"

I didn't say anything. I had gotten so moody and angry around my son-of-a-bitch father that Mom was too scared to tell me to clean my room.

She bit her bottom lip, and I could see the ghost of that frightened child. "It was right after I'd gotten Mr. Whiskers, too."

"Mr. Whiskers? That old cat? He was your pet way back then?"

"He was a stray that appeared on our doorstep one day. He took to me right away and wouldn't let me out of his sight."

"You mean..."

"Yes, he was my first familiar. Mom never cared for him. He would hiss at her if she got mad at me. Orson came along when Mr. Whiskers got old. He hung on long enough until I found Orson and to make sure I'd be okay with him."

"So that stupid cat that kept sleeping on my face, he helped you?"

"I still don't know how he found me. He guided me to a coven, and they helped me channel my abilities. And the coven helped me find Orson. I'm very grateful. My home life was so crazy. I don't know if I could have made it without them."

I nodded. The military was the perfect place for an angry young man to channel his rage at the world. I had no idea where a delicate, beautiful girl would have gone.

Sheila laughed. "I think Mr. Whiskers was a little jealous of you."

"I knew it!" The way he'd always half suffocated me with his tail at night had always seemed malicious.

"But don't be too hard on him. He didn't know if he could trust you."

"But Orson did."

"Yes, Orson always did. And so did I. Now you can make me an omelet."

"First things first." I leaned in to kiss her.

Orson snarfled and brought me out of my memories. His nose was buried in an empty McGriddle wrapper. He flashed me those baleful eyes.

I sighed. Again, I went through the blue folder. All I found were the same cryptic notes about Florida and the

Belly of the Beast. Sheila was an organized girl. She had kept receipts: a Jet Blue ticket from JFK to Jacksonville, an Avis car-rental contract, and a Mobil gas receipt. That Mobil station was across the street, but I didn't see anything special about it. I started the car and drove into the parking lot.

Inside, I didn't see anything unusual about the store, either. I picked up a map of Florida and took it to the counter.

"Don't sell many of these anymore," the clerk said. "Everyone just pulls out their phones for directions."

I told him I had really bad reception and didn't want to get lost in a swamp with no signal. The truth was that Sheila had made me ditch my phone soon after we started dating. Ramona was paranoid about cellphones, and she made sure no one in the coven owned one.

I had thought it was ridiculous. "Come on, Sheila. Who's tracking Ramona? Dorothy? The Tin Man?"

She gasped. "How did you know?" She laughed. "I'm sorry, but this is important to her, which means it's important to me. You know how she can get, and she's convinced people can track her through the phone."

I really couldn't argue, since we had done things like that in the army all the time. But I did miss playing *Angry Birds.*

I went back out to the car and spread the map out on the hood. We were currently near something called the Twelve Mile Swamp. *Delightful.* I figured a rental car would get about three hundred miles to a tank of gas. Since she filled up in Florida and not in Georgia, I guessed she went south then came back up to Jacksonville. Nearby was St. Augustine, and farther south were Daytona Beach and Cape Canaveral. Maybe the witches were going to colonize the moon.

I examined the tight little radius I hoped she had gone

to. Nothing popped out at me. If I had a phone, I could have Googled some of these places.

Orson nudged my boot. *Hungry.*

"You just ate."

An hour is not 'just ate.'

"I swear, you must have a tapeworm."

Please. So weak with hunger... Orson rolled over and played dead.

I rolled my eyes and went back into the gas station.

The attendant said, "Hello again, sir! Do you need a different map?"

Some sad-looking dried-up hot dogs lay on the grill beside the register. "Just give me two of those. No bun." I pointed at the door, where Orson was scratching himself outside. "They're for my dog."

"Oh! Well, then they're my treat. I was going to throw them out. Honestly, I would have talked you out of eating them. Those were on the grill from last night."

I shuddered and went to the door. Orson slobbered in expectation. Next to the exit was a display rack full of tourist pamphlets: Disney, Universal Studios, SeaWorld, plus some local attractions, like the Space Museum, Cocoa Beach, and a couple of alligator farms. I had an idea. I grabbed several for nearby places. Then I saw it. No, that couldn't be it.

"Your hot dogs, for your hot dog." The clerk chuckled at his joke.

"Thanks. Hey, how far is it to St. Augustine from here?"

"Not far at all. Less than half an hour. Have a drink of it for me, all right?"

"Yeah, sure." I left the store, hot dogs in one hand and brochures in the other. On top of the pile was a flier for the Fountain of Youth located in beautiful St. Augustine.

FOUR

THE SUN WAS HOT. THE buildings were old. Some had been spiffed up to be more artistically crumbly. The brochure said there were five hundred years of history there. I didn't much care.

Ponce de Leon had come in search of a fountain of youth. He found St. Augustine and a natural spring that, while I was sure was very refreshing after a few months of eating hardtack at sea, didn't prolong life expectancy. But who knew? Maybe Ramona wanted it to get rid of her crow's feet.

Orson buried his head in the fountain spring, slurping away. No one paid attention, although I was sure the other tourists wouldn't find the fountain of dog slobber quite so restorative.

I feel so young. I could go at it with a poodle all night.

"You feel like that every day."

Don't mess with success, cuz the best don't mess!

"Oh, yes, I forgot. You're the best." I scratched his head in that spot behind his ear that made his tongue loll out further.

He grinned like the Cheshire cat. *Hubba hubba! I smell one now!*

Through the gates, I could see a fluffy white poodle trotting down the pathway. I pulled Orson back lest he populate the earth with Bully Poos.

The fountain seemed like a dead end. I flagged down one of the park volunteers.

The portly retiree ambled over. "Hello! What can I help you with today?"

I showed him a photo of Sheila from last Christmas. She was beaming, her eyes lit up with joy. "This woman's gone missing, and she was last seen in the area. Can you tell me if she's been in here recently?"

"Sorry, I can't place her. A lot people come through. We get school trips in here all the time."

"Well, how's this? She was older than eight and over four feet tall."

"Lots of teachers, too. Sorry. She in trouble or something?"

"Or something. You don't remember any woman asking weird questions?"

"I get a lot of weird questions. Kids went to that last pirate movie and now they ask me about mermaid tears."

"Right." I took a breath so I wouldn't lose my patience. "Well, how about questions about the *real* fountain?"

"I get a lot of those, too. Some people are convinced we're hiding the real thing in a wading pool out back, keeping the cure for cancer to ourselves. I mean, the whole thing is a metaphor. The real fountain of youth is the Florida Coast. The fresh air, the sunshine, and beaches. Say, I have a cousin who can get you a good deal on a part-time beachfront residence."

I got away before Mr. Chamber of Commerce could con me into a time share.

I thumbed through the other brochures. Sheila hated car races and wet T-shirts, so Daytona was out. Beaches were an option. Maybe she was camped out in a motel along the coast. Maybe there was another coven here she was helping. If so, I didn't really know how to find them. If they were anything like the group in New York, they would be like hermits.

"Orson? Anything?"

No. No feeling for her, nothing— Orson suddenly jerked upright. His ears flattened back against his head, and he growled. Orson never growled unless it was serious.

I glanced around, but I didn't see anything that would cause his reaction. "What is it? What's wrong?"

Someone. Felt it before. Someone bad. He barked.

I spun around and saw a man in sunglasses and a loud Hawaiian shirt pivot away from us. He hesitated near the entrance, paying a lot of attention to the No Smoking sign. As I stared at him, he tried to nonchalantly slip out the door.

I gestured at the guy and asked Orson, "Him?"

Yes.

I started walking toward the guy, and he picked up his pace. He was fairly tall, and his legs covered some distance fast, but he was easy to track in his ugly shirt, which featured a bunch of neon parrots in sexually suggestive poses.

I hurried after him. If he had anything to do with Sheila being gone, I was going to find out. I'd beat the ugly out of his shirt if necessary.

He cast a glance over his shoulder then broke into a sprint, making a beeline for the parking lot. He ran through the handicapped parking area and toward the wall at the corner of the main complex. He ducked around the corner, which must have led to the rear, maybe to an employee parking lot.

Wait.

"I know." Some guy in a shirt so loud Helen Keller could have seen it just happened to be there the same day I had come there on a whim. Then he just happened to get spotted by me, and he ran away, toward the most isolated part of the parking lot. Mama didn't raise no dummies; I was heading right into a trap.

But that was encouraging. It meant I was on the right

path. I would just prefer not to run right into an ambush. But I couldn't leave without finding out some clues as to what was going on.

"Orson, head around back. See if there's a surprise party being planned for us."

Aye aye, Cap'n. Orson trotted off toward the delivery entrance.

I hugged the wall and poked my head around the corner. Ugly Shirt was still there, scuffing his feet on the ground, glancing back toward the direction he'd come from.

Two more. In the rear parking lot.

And there it was. "Okay, buddy. You ready for your *Cujo* audition?"

I was born to play it.

"Don't be afraid to go big."

I could feel the smirk from a hundred yards away. I burst around the corner and ran straight toward Ugly Shirt. Apparently expecting me, he hustled down the alley to the back parking lot.

"Hey, stop!" I yelled.

On cue, Orson sprang into action. He barked ferociously, driving the two goons into the alley. He snapped and lunged at the would-be attackers. Ugly Shirt stopped short. He spun around, and I grabbed him into a chokehold. I squeezed until he went down in a heap. Orson was holding his own, distracting the two rent-a-thugs, but I didn't want to take a chance that they weren't animal lovers.

Orson had latched onto one's pant leg, while the other tried to pull Orson off his buddy. They paid no attention to me as I came up behind them.

In Germany, a friend of mine had given me a blackjack, a round, leather-covered lead weight at the end of a six-inch handle, like a modified billy club. It was the spoils of victory from a bar fight. I always carried it with me because it came in quite handy, especially in situations like the one we were currently in. I cracked the first guy across the back of the skull, then the second, and they were out. The goons wouldn't be bothering anyone for a while. Not until after a fun hospital stay.

Orson was still drooling on one guy's pants.

"Down, Cujo."

What did you think?

"A little more foaming at the mouth next time. We have your headshot on file. We'll let you know."

Orson snorted then gave me his opinion of my critique by peeing on the unconscious attacker.

"When you're done, let's get to the car. We have a few things to ask Ugly Shirt."

FIVE

I PILED UGLY SHIRT INTO THE back of the car then drove a few miles south and parked under a quiet highway overpass. "Wake up."

Ugly Shirt didn't move. He was going bald in the front. The acne and broad shoulders made me think he might be a juicer. The man shouldn't have been out so long from a stupid chokehold.

I slapped Ugly Shirt, and he twitched but didn't wake. "Ready for the callback?"

Orson grinned.

I hauled back and slapped Ugly Shirt hard. His skin was sweaty and greasy. *Ew.* "Wake up, jackass!"

Orson barked.

Ugly Shirt slowly came around, groaning and blinking. When he saw Orson snarling and me scowling, he roused in a hurry. "What...?"

Orson growled.

"Shut up. Don't talk. Don't move." I gestured at Orson. "You get one chance, then I let my friend here have dinner. He's awfully hungry."

Orson growled again, showing his teeth. Ugly Shirt flinched.

"Why were you waiting for me at the fountain?" I asked him.

"I don't know what you're talking about! I was just out for a walk, and I—"

Orson snapped at him, coming very close to the guy's neck. Ugly Shirt tried to squirm backward but bumped against the car door.

"Wrong answer. One more shot and then I don't hold him back."

"Hey, I don't know—"

Orson lunged, and I really did have to pull him back. "Down!"

Ugly Shirt cringed. "Okay! Okay! All I know is, a couple days ago, some guy came to my gym." *Yep. Steroid acne.* "He told me and the guys he'd pay us a grand each to hang out at the fountain. He said a guy with a bulldog would be coming there soon."

"What did he want with me?"

He smirked. "You? Nothing. He didn't care about you. He said to tune you up and take the dog."

What is he talking about? Orson asked.

I shrugged. "You got beat up for an attempted dognapping?"

Orson barked, pulling at the hold I still had on him, and tried to claw at the guy some more. *Yeah, what the hell? And you'd better send more than three guys next time! And where's Mama?*

"Yeah, where's his mama?" I asked the guy.

Ugly Shirt frowned. "Mama? Whose mama?"

Oh, right. Not everyone can hear Orson. "Did that guy say anything about a woman? Did he have someone with him?"

"No. He was alone. He did say you might be trying to find a girl. Someone named Sheila."

That really made Orson snarl and bite. I had to pull back on his leash, hard. "Down!"

The would-be tough guy tried to cover his face.

"What were you supposed to do when you got the dog?" I asked.

"He gave us a number to call! Keep him off me! The number's in my pocket."

I held out my hand. Ugly Shirt jabbed his hand into his back pocket and pulled out a business card. I took it and flipped it over in my hand. The card was blank except for a handwritten number. I didn't recognize it. "What did this guy look like?"

"I don't know."

"Don't push it."

"I mean it! I don't know!"

"You talked to him. Right, dummy?"

"I know, but I... I can't remember!" His eyes were like saucers and full of fear and panic. Maybe he was serious.

Orson stared at him for a second. *He doesn't remember. That thought's been blurred out.*

Interesting. And a little scary. I didn't know if that was a common thing among magical people. Sheila hadn't mentioned it. "Well, my friend, you present an interesting puzzle for us."

He stared at me like the dumb, confused animal he was.

"I can't have you warning this man that we're coming. And I can't have you running around blabbing in general."

"I won't say anything! I swear!"

"Oh, I know." I released my grip on Orson. "You're up, pal."

Orson growled at him, eyes glowing. His growl slowly eased into a purr.

"You hear me?"

Ugly Shirt relaxed. "Yessss..."

It was a fun party trick. One time, I was about to scream at a parking cop, which would have certainly gotten me arrested or tased, when Sheila had Orson do his thing. The cop tore up the ticket, and he didn't seem to remember a thing as he strolled away.

"Here's the deal. Call the number. Tell the man you have the dog. Ask him where to bring it."

"Okaaaay...." He pulled out his phone.

I reached out and pressed the button to put it on speaker. It rang a long time.

A man answered, "Hello?" The voice sounded young, as if the owner was trying to come across as important.

"We did it. We have the dog."

"About time. Bring it to me."

"Where?"

"Tomorrow, twelve p.m. The rest stop on 95 South, near mile marker 300."

"Okaaaaayy..."

The stranger hung up.

"Very good," I said. "Now, one more thing. Go find your friends. Tell them it's done whenever they wake up. Then forget you ever met us."

"Okaaayy..."

I pointed down across the parking lot. "St. Augustine is five miles that way. Get going." I gave him a shove for good measure. Once he was out of earshot, I asked Orson, "He's not going to remember a thing, is he?"

No. But you should have let me bite him anyway.

"He was plenty scared."

There are principles involved.

"We got what we needed. We're one step closer. We find his boss, and we get closer to Sheila."

Yes.

"Come on. We're getting there," I said in response to his grouchy tone. "Hey, there was a burger joint back there. You haven't eaten in at least three hours. Hungry?"

Orson seemed sullen and didn't answer, which was unusual when food was mentioned. I drove to the hamburger stand. After I ordered the food, we sat on the hood of the car. Orson barely paid attention to the double chili cheeseburger I put in front of him.

"How did he see you?" I finally asked. "Nobody sees you unless you want them to. How did that meatstick do it?"

People ignore me if they aren't looking for me. He was. That takes more effort. I wasn't expecting it.

"Well, start expecting it. Eat up. You'll need your energy."

Orson sat there like a lump.

"What's wrong? We're closer now than we've ever been."

Not hungry.

"You're never not hungry." I tried to pet him, but he shrugged me off. "What is it?"

If she's here, I'll feel her.

"Right."

Can't feel her. Why won't she let me?

I had spent so long worrying about Sheila and thinking about how much I missed her, I forgot that Orson would miss her just as much. The familiar link went both ways.

I leaned over and put my forehead on his. His fur was warm and soft. "I know."

Orson whimpered.

"I know. She hasn't tried to call me, either. All I can think is that she must be in serious trouble. I know how much she loves you. If she's had to hide, it must be serious for her not to reach out to you." I stroked Orson's back. It wasn't as furry as it had been a week ago. Maybe he was shedding in the heat. Sure. That was it. "We just have to keep trying until we can't try anymore. I can barely breathe without her near. I can't imagine how you must feel."

You are all she thinks about.

"You are all she talks about."

Orson licked my cheek. His rough tongue licked away the tear I didn't know was there. *You going to finish that burger?*

SIX

THE REST STOP WAS BUSY. It was the last one before the exit to Orlando. Minivans and RVs full of families had pulled off to use the restroom and buy drinks before they finished their trip to Disney World. I counted at least four people strolling around with pets. With so much coming and going and children shouting, a little scuffle with a would-be dognapper would go unnoticed.

We had gotten there at nine that morning and parked in a far corner of the lot in order to scope things out. We were obviously at a disadvantage. The mystery man knew what his lackey looked like. We didn't know what to expect. A little attention was fine, but if things went south, we'd need some space to work. Ideally, we would grab the guy and find out what he knew.

Orson was going to have to do the heavy lifting in the operation. He sat up in the passenger seat. I put on sunglasses, reclined the driver's seat all the way back, and pretended to nap. Since Ugly Shirt had been propositioned at the gym, I hoped Mr. Mysterious didn't know what kind of car to expect. Orson would sense him before he got too close. Hopefully, Orson would also sense if the guy had brought any backup. I didn't expect any trouble. It was just a simple exchange: Orson for money. Still, I had no idea what we were dealing with, since Mr. Shirt couldn't tell us anything about him.

Maybe you should've kept that loser around.

"Maybe I would've if I could keep you from biting him every ten seconds."

Touché.

I checked my watch: eleven thirty. I didn't expect the guy to be late. I thought he would have gotten here early. I just hoped we had been earlier. It would have been even better if I could have been watching from a distance, but it would be too suspicious looking if I left Orson alone in the car. I didn't see anyone carrying an Evil Mastermind sign, so all I could do was stay loose and ready for whatever came.

I tried to relax and center myself by taking deep breaths. Sheila had taught me about energy and how to focus and meditate. I had been so full of anger when we met. Angry at my family. Angry at being sent to Iraq. Angry at the Iraqis for shooting at me. Angry at just about anyone who looked at me cross-eyed. My unit used to call me Banner. "Don't get Banner angry. You wouldn't like him when he's angry." Then they'd pump me full of tequila and turn me loose on a table of unsuspecting locals.

Somehow, Sheila looked past all of my rage and tried to bring out the person she saw inside me. She taught me how to get it under control, although the first lessons hadn't gone very well.

"Now, I want you to start with breathing."

I smirked. "Well, of course."

Sheila sighed and lit a candle. "I need you to take this seriously. It's important. You can't walk Orson if I think you're going to pick a fight with every pit bull owner who gives you attitude."

"It was a sixty-pound mastiff! And he didn't have him on a leash!"

"Orson can take care of himself better than you think. And what were you going to do to the owner? He was a kid! One punch and you could have killed him!"

"But—"

Sheila held up her hand. "I know you've been through a lot. So have I. The reason I can function, the reason I don't shake with rage every minute of the day, is because I learned how to focus and meditate. Whenever I have a problem I can't solve, whenever Ramona makes too many demands, whenever the people I care about cause problems"—she glared at me—"I meditate. Now, start with breathing."

I breathed. It seemed a little dumb, but Sheila always knew what she was doing.

She coached me well. "Every time you breathe out, you breathe out whatever is bothering you. Breathe out the anger."

Whooosh.

"Breathe out the frustration."

Whooosh.

Each deep inhale brought the scent of the sandalwood candle and a little loosening of my tension. It took a while, but I learned how to relax. I'd always assumed that relaxed meant sleepy or foggy. But for the first time in thirty years, I felt my shoulders unclench. Relaxed meant aware, alert, and focused.

Orson chuffed and cocked his head. *Something.*

I glanced up at him. "Is it him?"

I feel... blackness. It must be. Orson was staring across the lot. I tried to peek over the door, but I couldn't see too much without giving myself away.

"Alone?"

Think so. Hard to focus.

I slipped the blackjack out of my pocket and hid it under my arm. The sounds of the rest stop seemed to recede. The tire squeals, the engine revs, the children laughing and screaming all faded. I could only hear the sound of boots on pavement.

The steps weren't hurried. They were measured and confident, purposeful. And they were getting closer. I shivered. Even in the warm noonday sun, I felt a chill. Orson whimpered. I hoped he was just playing his part. In the driver-side mirror, I spotted a guy approaching the rear of the car. Despite the almost ninety-degree weather, he was dressed in all black, with long, stringy black hair.

"Finally." The guy's voice was smooth, but it had an edge of sharp glass in it. He came up to the passenger door and leaned into the open window, eyes locked on Orson, who shrank into the seat cushion. The guy didn't even notice me until he got within arm's reach. "Hey, you aren't—"

I sprang up and grabbed his shirt with my left hand. Pulling him toward me, I cracked him across the temple with the blackjack in my right hand. He grunted, going limp in my grip as he blinked, dazed. I became aware of the sounds of activity starting up again.

Orson shook his head and growled. I wrestled the guy over the front seats and into the back, not releasing my blackjack in case he rallied enough to cause a problem. His head wound up on the floor in front of Orson's seat. One of his feet caught on the window ledge and was sticking out of the car, twitching as the guy tried to regain his bearings. I reached over to pull his leg back in the car. I'd just have to sic Orson on him if he recovered while we were driving.

"Hey, what are you doing?"

Oh great. Some kid walking a Great Dane was coming our way. It would be tough to explain the current situation to a state trooper. I yanked the guy's leg into the car and dropped back into my seat. I started the car and slammed it into reverse. I backed out slowly enough so as not to kill the kid but quickly enough that he had to jump out of the way, hopefully without having time to read my license plate. His dog barked, and Orson responded in kind.

When I got us back on the highway, I glanced over at

Orson. He looked a little shaken up, hunched up in his seat. "You okay?" I asked him.

He grunted. *Fine. Find a place to work on this guy.*

"It would be my absolute pleasure."

SEVEN

I DIDN'T WANT TO LINGER ON the highway. If that kid decided to call the police, I wanted to be well out of sight. I pulled off two exits down and found a shuttered condo development. Weeds had cracked through the pavement in a few spots, and a For Sale or Lease sign was posted in the front yard. The place was probably a victim of the real-estate crash. From the rust on the chain across the driveway, it had been a long time since anyone had visited, so the building was perfect for our purposes.

Do not go easy on him.

"That all depends on him. Remember, he can't tell us where Sheila is if you tear out his throat."

Orson glared at me. *If he did anything to her, you won't stop me.*

"If he did anything to her, you'll have to get in line. But he has to talk first, okay?"

I was once a Boy Scout, long ago in another life, and I took the Be Prepared motto seriously. I always carried rope and duct tape in the trunk. Using most of a roll of duct tape, we trussed up the Man in Black as he continued to groan. Hopefully, I hadn't hit him so hard he'd be useless. We found two palm trees a few feet apart, stood him between them, and tied his taped hands to one and his taped feet to the other.

He was in his early twenties and had probably dressed the way he thought a badass magic man should dress, provided that badass magic man hit the Hot Topic at the Galleria. He had pale white skin, the kind one got from living in Mom's basement or from pancake makeup. I was almost surprised that black dye didn't come off on my hand when I touched his head. But his hair was just naturally black and greasy.

Still, he had some ability. If he could befuddle those halfwits from St. Augustine, he had to know something. And if he gave Orson the creeps with his black aura, that meant he had some training.

"Get him to focus," I told Orson.

Orson scampered over, lifted his leg, and peed on Hot Topic's face.

The guy spluttered and gagged. "Get away, foul beast!"

I rolled my eyes. He had obviously taken the badass-magician vocabulary lessons. "You're pretty foul yourself. You may not have noticed, but you're in no position to boss anyone around."

"You dare to address me in this fashion?" A slight slur undermined his effort to sound intimidating. Obviously, he was still recovering from that blow to the head. "Do you not know who you are dealing with?"

"Yes, I dare. And as to who I am addressing, why don't you enlighten me, O Dark and Powerful Nitwit?"

He stared at me and furrowed his brow. He concentrated on me so hard, I was afraid he might crap himself.

I asked Orson, "Is he doing what I think he's doing?"

I think he's trying to cast a spell. Not succeeding. He's not going to surprise me this time. Orson was a very useful friend to have.

Hot Topic yanked at the ropes. "Untie me!"

Orson and I shared a puzzled glance. "No."

The guy looked stunned—and I didn't think it was from a knock to the head. He'd really expected that to work. He wiggled his fingers a little, and his eyes opened wide. "Give it back!"

"Give what back? And where do you get off ordering us around?"

He sputtered, and his white face became tinged with purple. "You do not know what you are meddling in!"

Sheila had told me about the wannabes, misfits who wanted to believe in something magical and bigger than themselves. If they were lucky, they wound up in a basement with other like-minded people playing Cure records, drinking absinthe, and talking about the Book of Shadows. Then they would graduate from high school and realize the rest of the world was better than the crap show where they'd just spent four years.

If they were unlucky, they bumped into some nasty people, ones who could teach them a parlor trick or two and convince them they were big, scary magic men. Those people wouldn't be afraid to use the sad clowns to do their dirty work. Hot Topic had no idea just how unlucky he was.

I shook my head. "I've got a pretty good idea, slick. Some dark and mysterious man found you brooding at the mall. He told you that you were meant for greater things. He taught you a couple of things, like how to make idiots forget about seeing you. Now, you think you're a dark lord of the Sith or something and that makes you King Shit. How we doing so far?"

Hot Topic seethed. At least he stopped with the melodramatic pronouncements. He was getting good and angry. I hoped he would get so mad that he let something slip.

"And wow, you must be super important to the Dark Lord of Douchebags, or whatever stupid name he's calling himself. He sent you all the way here to pick up a little bulldog. Yet you managed to fuck that up. We must be scraping the bottom of the barrel for flunkies. Maybe your dad was right about you after all."

His face was mottled with rage. He tried to jerk forward. "You know nothing of Yareth's plans! That dog is key!"

I shot a glance at Orson. *Something you're not telling me?*

Orson tilted his head. *News to me.*

"So, Yareth? He's the mastermind behind all this?"

Hot Topic didn't respond.

"What does Yareth want with the dog?"

"He did not say." The slurring had entirely worn off. "It is not my place to question him. When he commands Malvolio, it is my privilege to obey."

I snickered. "Malvolio?"

"Yes. It is a historic name that portends great chaos and malevolence."

"No, it's a comic-relief buffoon from *Twelfth Night*. For a goth kid, you sure don't read much." I ignored his glare. "What's your real name?"

"Malvolio is my real name now! Yareth granted it to me in a sacred rite of—"

I kneed him in the side to shut him up then slipped his wallet out of his back pocket. I smirked as I peeled back the Velcro to uncover his driver's license. "Mortimer Morrison? Damn, I'd call myself Malvolio, too, with a name like that."

"Give that back!"

"Sure." I tucked his wallet into my front shirt pocket, then I got out my own wallet and pulled out a photo of Sheila. I held it up in front of his face. "Have you seen her? Is she part of the plan?"

Mortimer snorted. "That bitch is insignificant. A mere obstacle on the path of—"

Orson lunged, snapping and snarling. I made no effort to pull him back as he bit at the wriggling little acolyte's ankles. Flecks of spittle flew from Orson's jowls.

I waggled a finger at the guy. "I'd step very carefully if I were you. Don't talk bad about his mama."

Orson stepped back but issued a warning growl. Mortimer tried to get as far away from Orson as he could, which wasn't very far.

"Again. When did you see her? What did you do to her?"

"I have said too much already." He tried to smirk. He was putting up a brave face, but his eyes were too wide and scared to pull it off.

Making Morty angry would only get us so far. I decided fear might be a better motivator.

"You know, funny thing about these condos. They have such colorful names. Panther Valley. Pelican Bay. You know what this one was called? Gator Gulch."

Hot Topic sneered. "So what?"

"So that usually means they paved over some swampland to build these homes on. And since no one has bought one, that means the former residents are moving back in. They're probably really hungry to meet a guy of your talents."

Orson growled, his eyes glowing red and gold. Behind the trees that edged the yard, the tall grass rustled. A scaly snout with beady eyes appeared. Then another. And another. Three six-foot gators crawled toward the trussed-up goth. Morty gasped.

"So, scary magic man, is the great and powerful Yareth going to teleport you away from the gators? Or are you gonna tell me what I want to know?"

As he gaped at the alligators coming his way, his skin turned even whiter, which I wouldn't have thought possible. "You can't do this!" He struggled against the rope and tape. "You aren't going to get me to talk!"

"Oh, well. We tried. Come on, boy!"

Orson and I headed toward the car. The gators inched closer. They were maybe fifteen feet away.

"Wh-Where are you going?"

"To find Yareth. Can't be too many of them in Florida. See you round, Morty."

"Wait!"

Orson and I looked back at him. He was thrashing desperately to loosen the tape. The gators were getting pretty close.

"You got something to say?" I asked.

"I saw her, okay? I saw her."

"When?"

"Two weeks ago! I went by Yareth's place. And they were arguing. She was furious. Yareth just smirked at her. She screamed at him that this wasn't over, and then she stormed out. She almost knocked me down."

Orson growled. I felt like doing that myself.

"So where is she now?" I asked.

"I don't know!"

"Where do we find Yareth?"

"I don't know!"

I ground my teeth. The gators were only a few feet away. Orson's eyes were still flashing gold as he kept up the growl.

"I don't! I swear! He cast something that made me forget the address. I can only find it if he wants me to be there."

"What does he want with the dog?"

"I don't know! Please, believe me, I don't!"

Orson bobbed his head. The guy wasn't lying. That was all we were going to get out of him.

Damn it. "Thanks, Mortimer. You've been *so* helpful. But you should really be more careful about who you associate with. It might get you in trouble one day." I turned and continued walking back to the car.

"Wait! I told you everything! You can't leave me here!"

"You say that a lot," I called over my shoulder.

"We had a deal! Call them off!"

I reached the car door and looked back at him. The gators slithered closer to their dinner. One of them snapped dramatically at Morty's left foot.

"That's not my doing." I patted Orson on the head. "And

even if I wanted to, I don't think I could get him to do that. And you know what? I don't want to."

Morty started crying. A snot bubble blew out from his nose. I rolled my eyes. *What a pathetic, stupid kid.* But I had been a stupid kid once. I nudged Orson and nodded at him. He growled and shook his head.

"Do it."

He whined but blinked. His eyes lost the gold, and the gators stopped their march on Morty.

I grabbed a box cutter from the car and marched back to the sobbing sorcerer. "Tell you what. You did help us, so here's a little present." I placed the handle of the cutter a couple of inches from his fingertips. "Gators don't usually move too much. They just like to lie in the sun." I gestured at the sky. "But the sun will go down." I returned to where Orson, tail wagging, stood beside the car. I could hear Morty grunting as he strained to reach the knife.

I opened the door for Orson. "You know, I didn't know you could do that. Summon animals and all."

What you don't know... He hopped into the passenger seat.

"Just like Aquaman and the fishes."

Orson's upper lip lifted to show teeth, the doggie equivalent of a scowl. *Aquaman is so lame.*

EIGHT

NOT HAVING A CELL PHONE certainly had benefits. The government couldn't track me. No telemarketers could call me. I didn't have to worry about roaming charges or fake "unlimited" data plans. I saved six hundred dollars a year.

Of course, if I was in the middle of Florida swampland and needed to call New York, I wasn't going to have much luck. Pay phones were going the way of vinyl LPs and smoking sections in restaurants.

How old are you, Grandpa?

"Nice, Orson. Hope you don't pull my plug when I'm in the home."

We finally found a working pay phone at a gas station off of I-4. I dug all of the change out of the ashtray and plunked the coins into the slot.

Lisa answered on the third ring. "Gabriel! Did you find her?"

"Not yet, but it's promising. You didn't hear from her, did you?"

"No."

"Okay. Listen, did you ever hear of someone in Florida named Yareth? Some kind of dark magic user. He has some followers, thinks he's a big deal?"

"Yareth? No, never."

"According to a reliable source, he's the last person to have seen Sheila."

"How reliable?"

"Stake his life on it. This source says they were having a shouting match about two weeks back. Said she almost bowled him over, storming away from the Yareth guy. Have you ever known Sheila to knock over anyone? She'll go out of her way to step around an ant."

Lisa didn't respond.

"Are you sure this has nothing to do with whatever it was you sent her for?" I prodded. "It seems awfully coincidental that she goes to his lair and then disappears right after you send her down here."

She stayed quiet.

"So you really want to tell me that you've never heard of this Yareth character?"

"I haven't. I really haven't. But I'll ask the coven." She sounded sincere, but I wasn't sure I believed her.

"You do that. I'm going to keep looking for your best friend."

"Gabriel! That's not fair."

"If you want to help me, we can talk about fair. I'll call you later." I hung up.

Stupid coven nonsense. Someone in that nest knew who Yareth was. He probably had whatever it was the coven wanted, which might be Orson.

Orson scratched his ear and yawned. *Nice to be wanted. I'm a catch.*

We got back in the car and headed down the highway. Morty's wallet had provided more than his name. The three grand he had promised the thugs in St. Augustine was also in there. I was surprised. I thought he would have just taken the dog and magicked the memory of the exchange out of their heads. Maybe he would have done that and kept Yareth's money. Honor among thieves was a myth.

The license had an address, probably his mom's. I decided we might get a lead on Yareth there.

The sun was getting low in the sky, and the glare caused the west-bound traffic to slow to a crawl. We passed a sign that read: Welcome to Orlando.

I shuddered.

NINE

ORLANDO HAD MANY FABULOUS RESORTS and hotels that catered to vacationing families, and a lot of them were located in and around theme parks. They were also quite expensive. Even with the unexpected bounty of Morty's three grand, I thought it best to go cheap and keep a low profile. It wouldn't be smart to check in with a dog at Mickey's Vacation Paradise and talk to everyone about dark magic and witches. Maybe we could say we were remaking Snow White. Orson was really a new dwarf named Drooly.

Getting off the highway, we headed away from the resorts and theme parks. We drove down a road featuring a long strip of chain restaurants, all-you-can-eat buffets, and billboards for lesser-known attractions, many touting mini-golf or alligators. It was like a bunch of lampreys feeding off a shark in mouse ears.

There were also a ton of lower-end hotels. The signs didn't come right out and say it, but the unspoken pitch was "save your money for the theme parks!" The farther from the parks we got, the cheaper the rates became.

Orson yawned. It had been a long day, what with threatening teenagers with alligators and all. If we did stumble onto Yareth at Morty's mom's house, we would be in no shape to deal with him. I pulled into the lot of a motel called the Kingdom of Magic. That was probably as close as they could get to the real thing without being sued. The three-story affair was purple, and the paint was sun faded and chipped in places. The purple neon trim was lighting up as I approached the front desk. I had only ever seen purple neon at strip clubs. Maybe there had been a sale.

The woman at the front desk was chain smoking, and with her tan and leathery face, she could have been anywhere from thirty-five to sixty. *Maybe she should visit the Florida coast and enjoy its restorative qualities.* I asked for a room.

"I'll see what I have."

Gee, I hoped there was room. There had been maybe three cars in the lot when I pulled in.

She pretended to examine the register for a minute. "Single rate is $32.95 a night, $159 a week."

This was the last place anyone had seen Sheila. I was willing to spend a few days covering every square inch of theme park if I had to. "I'll take a week." I took two hundreds out of my pocket.

She made change, two twenties and a one. "I'll need a credit card for a room deposit."

I slid a twenty back toward her. "No, you don't."

"And a copy of your license."

The other twenty went across the desk. She shrugged. I guessed mine was not an uncommon request.

"No pets."

There was a can on the desk asking for donations to the ASPCA. That got the last dollar.

"No problem. Ground floor, please." I liked being able to park in front of my room. Quicker all around.

She gave me a plastic room card. "Room 117. Weeklies get maid service twice a week, Tuesday and Friday."

When I made it around the side of the motel and inside, I saw Room 117 needed a lot more maid service than twice a week. Twice a day with a hazmat crew and a blowtorch might have helped. The room was damp and dingy, and with the shades drawn to keep out the ugly orange light from the parking lot, the weak little desk lamp barely penetrated the gloom. The bed sagged in the middle. We checked the mattress for bedbugs, and fortunately, there were none. It was hard to be intimidating while frantically scratching.

Orson whined as he leapt onto the bed. *Call the shelter. There's an abused dog here.*

"Quiet."

I flipped on the TV just to get some white noise in the room. I found a *Law & Order* marathon.

Jerry Orbach was staring at a gurney as the paramedics wheeled away a dead hooker. "I guess her trick was no treat," he quipped.

Orson chuffed with contentment. He was a big fan of Jerry Orbach.

I risked hepatitis and sat down in the ugly armchair. Closing my eyes, I reviewed everything I knew.

Four weeks ago, Sheila had been sent by the coven to the Jacksonville area to find... something. Three weeks ago, she returned to New York, upset and out of sorts. Two weeks ago, she disappeared without a trace. She took the roll of bills she kept hidden in her bedroom. I had a friend from the army who had become a cop. He put an alert on her credit cards, but there had been no activity on them. She had maxed out the daily withdrawal limit on her ATM card the day she left then not touched it again.

She wound up at Yareth's House of Mystery, where she screamed at him then stormed out. Meanwhile, I started asking about her whereabouts, and Lisa finally gave me a hint as to where Sheila had gone. After I followed the breadcrumbs and wound up in Florida, I got beset by inept thugs who had been told a week in advance that I was coming. Sheila had made me believe in magic, but I had my doubts that Yareth could feel a tremor in the force from that distance. Unless the tremor was a phone call. From Lisa. Or maybe from someone else in the coven.

That was problematic. I had just told Lisa that I was going to see Yareth. If the coven really was feeding him information, I might as well have hired a skywriter. Still, I didn't have any options. I had one lead, and it led to Morty's gothic basement.

The only other choice was quitting. That was no choice at all.

I opened my eyes. Jerry Orbach was in the police station. Jerry wouldn't quit, either. He was reading an autopsy report. "He had three kinds of semen in his stomach. Must have been at a buffet."

Orson was staring at me, dolefully. *I'm hungry.*

TEN

THE NEXT MORNING, WE WENT to the suburban tract home that had spawned young Malvolio. I was wrong about one thing. There was no basement in the ranch house. Everything else was pretty much as I expected.

We got there early and waited at the end of the block. Just after seven o'clock, the garage door rolled up, and a beige Accord backed out. The car turned in the opposite direction, to the left. With the windows tinted against the Florida sun, I couldn't see much, just a hint of blond hair, which I assumed belong to Morty's mother. I did notice that there were no other cars in the garage, so Morty probably hadn't gotten free of the gators yet.

We waited for thirty minutes after the car was out of sight to make sure no one else was home or that the woman wouldn't immediately return. The back door had a simple lock, and a quick bark from Orson scrambled the alarm system keypad.

The interior of the house was the picture of middle-class suburbia: tidy living room, combined kitchen and dining room, and two bedrooms. The neat one with the clothes hung up in the closet was obviously the mother's.

The one painted all black had to be Morty's.

Drawn in chalk on the wall above the head of the bed was a pentagram. *Check.* A dog-eared copy of the *Satanic Bible* lay on the nightstand. *Check.* Lots of candles were scattered around the room. *Check.* Apparently, no cliché would be left unturned.

His laptop sat on his desk, between two resin skulls with candles sprouting from their tops. *Oh, hardcore.* I powered up the laptop. Orson perched by the door, ready to pounce should Morty come staggering into the room. Orson let out a tongue-curling yawn.

The startup screen asked for a password. The username had been saved: Malvolio, of course. I could have had Orson get me into the system, but his bark could sometimes totally fry more delicate electronics.

Hmmm... Initial instincts were usually the best. I tried the first thing that came to mind: Yareth. No luck. Some password software required the user to add numbers and special characters. I tried Yareth#1. *No.* If I didn't get in on the third try, I might get locked out. Then I remembered an officer in the army who had kept missile launch codes under his desk blotter. Super tight security. Morty didn't have a desk blotter, so I checked under the laptop. I spotted a little square of paper taped to the bottom with "Yareth#One!" written on it. I had been so close.

I poked through the computer files. There wasn't much there. His browser history showed a taste for porn sites that featured tattooed girls with piercings, long black hair, and bored expressions. His hard drive held mostly music and videos. I definitely didn't see a text file labeled "Yareth's Hiding Place!" or "Missing Girl FAQ."

I scrolled through his photo galleries. There were a few hundred pictures, and when I scrolled fast enough, it was like riffling through one of those flip books I had as a kid. The boy's hair got longer and darker, his skin got whiter, and his smile became a scowl.

I didn't think there would be a photo of Yareth, considering all the trouble he went through to keep his location hidden from his acolytes, but I checked, anyway. He probably wouldn't be in a front-facing headshot, so

I scrolled to an album with some pictures of a party that appeared to have been held in a dark night club. In one photo, Morty had his arm around a skinny goth girl. Both were smiling in a way that made them appear vaguely amused rather than happy. Behind them in the background was an older man, maybe in his late thirties or early forties. His hair was long, and he had a neatly trimmed goatee waxed to a sharp point. That could be Yareth. The time stamp was only a few months old. I printed the picture.

While I waited for the printer to finish, I checked under Morty's mattress, the number-one hiding place for *Playboys* and naughty contraband. Nothing. I checked in his closet and his dresser. More nothing. The nightstand had a blacklight lamp and a pentagram pendant. On closer inspection, I noticed that the sides of the pentagram were naked ladies stretched out and contorted in odd positions. *Classy.* I pulled out the drawers of his desk and checked for anything taped underneath them. Nothing.

That stupid kid was my only lead. *I should track him down again and throw him back to the gators.*

I imagined Sheila's voice in my head. *Focus. Stay calm.*

Orson whimpered. He didn't like to see me get angry.

I closed my eyes and took a few deep breaths. *Whoosh. Whoosh.* My heart rate calmed. There had to be something here. Mom probably wasn't coming back until five. We had time. We would find it.

I started to put the drawers back in the desk. As I did, I noticed a few colored envelopes marked with "City of Orlando." I pulled out the contents: five parking tickets. Apparently, minions of Yareth were forbidden to carry quarters for parking meters. Three of the tickets were from violations on the same street: Edgewater Drive. That was definitely a potential lead.

Orson chuffed and walked over to the nightstand. He nudged it with the side of his head. I pushed the small table away from the bed. A ring lay on the floor. It was big and wide with a dark purple stone, like a school ring, but no school I knew of had a motto like the one engraved on the inside. *Live to Serve, Sacrifice to Live.* Weird.

When the photo finished printing, I took it and the ring. Maybe it was Yareth's secret decoder ring. One more breadcrumb. It was something, anyway. *Get enough, and we could make toast.*

Orson cocked his head. *What does that even mean?*

Everyone's a critic.

ELEVEN

EDGEWATER DRIVE WAS NOWHERE NEAR water. I wasn't exactly shocked. I was more surprised that it was a fairly upscale street. North and west of downtown, the neighborhood was a mix of pastel condos and boutique stores, like art galleries, and designer scarf shops. I'd been expecting something seedier.

As I drove down the street, Orson perked up every time we passed a shop selling gourmet dog treats, which was often. I scanned for the addresses listed on the tickets. One was in front of a 7-Eleven, the second was in front of a dress shop where all the dresses seemed to be made out of quilt squares, and the last one was on the next block in front of a gym. At the center of it all was a new age shop. The coven in New York was based in a new age store. Maybe whatever group Yareth had was as well.

I pointed at the sign. "That seems like a good bet."

Orson made a mental scoffing sound. *No. Nothing there.*

"What? It's perfect cover! We should go in."

Not unless you need some patchouli. No presence. No.

I sighed. He could pick up on things. All his senses were sharp, especially the ones I didn't have.

Orson jerked his head to the left. *There.*

I turned and saw a consignment store on the corner. It was the kind that sold used jeans for three hundred dollars. "You feel something?"

Orson seemed very agitated. *No.* He pressed his nose against the car window.

"Then why...?"

I don't feel anything. At all. Shields.

I understood. When I was a kid, I read a Superman comic where some gangsters had kidnapped Lois Lane. Again. They told Superman he would never find her because she was in a lead-lined room, and Superman's x-ray vision couldn't see through lead. Of course, Superman just scanned the city until he found a room he couldn't see into, then he burst in and saved Lois. And he got a chaste kiss for his trouble while Lois got another scoop.

I drove down the street and parked a few blocks away. There was no point in us being conspicuous. If Sheila's coven really was in contact with Yareth, they might have told him what I was driving. I got out and put in enough change for a full hour on the meter.

Orson hopped out of the car, but I pointed back at it. "No. Stay here!"

What? No! He circled my legs and tried to nudge me forward with his wet nose.

"Think. If they're looking for you, how stupid would it be to walk right into their home?"

Like you're doing?

"We both know you're the smart one. Besides, you remember what Morty said. You're the key. I'm insignificant."

You have significance. You need to feed me. Besides, you leaving me alone is probably what they want. It's okay. I can take them. I have permission to bite them, right? Lemme at 'em! Lemme at 'em! He did his best Cowardly Lion impression.

That one always got me. I chuckled and scratched his ear in the spot that made his leg go crazy. Orson grinned, and his tongue lolled in a silly grimace.

I closed the convertible top and put him in the backseat.

"Stay out of sight. Behave, and we'll go to the doggie bakery."

Orson growled, but he nestled down on the floor. *You're no fun! I'm telling Mom!*

"Yeah, well, sue me."

I closed the door and jogged across the street to the store entrance. I would have rather it had been the new age shop. I had spent enough time in them, waiting for Sheila, that I was used to them and the odd smell of incense. I had gone into a consignment store in the East Village once to find a present for Sheila. It took the staff ten minutes to notice me and another ten before they would deign to talk to me. Then they tried to sell me a sweater with holes in it for two hundred dollars. Hopefully, the clerks in this place would have the same attitude. It would give me some time to check the place out and see if there were any signs that Sheila had been there or some hint that Yareth was holding court in the joint. Maybe there would even be something nice and obvious, like a trail of pentagrams.

"Good morning! Welcome to Clothes of Future Passed!" The older, yet wholesomely pretty, clerk smiled at me with all her teeth. "Can I help you find anything?"

Oh well. People were friendlier down south. "Uh... just browsing."

"Well, you let me know if there's anything I can do for you!"

It was way too early for aggressively cheerful. Actually, I didn't think it was ever late enough for aggressively cheerful. I missed the rude shop girls of Soho. I nodded to her and wandered down an aisle lined with shelves of distressed jeans. Unfortunately, I was the only one there. With a clerk that cheery, there would be no way for me to slip into the back, and I didn't think I could stall until more people came in.

The store was supposed to be a cool and funky place, but it was trying a little too hard, just like the clerk. It was odd they would be so intense about making you relax, but then I found most fashionable stores odd. Most of the clothes I had from childhood through high school had come from the Salvation Army or church rummage sales. And once I joined the army, they took care of the wardrobe. I had always felt it was a waste to spend more than ten dollars on any article of clothing. Sheila had gotten me a suit jacket for my birthday, and the thing had cost more than my first month of army pay. I was going to tell her to take it back, but she made me put it on, and then I understood why concepts like "fabric" and "tailoring" were important and why maybe the expensive jacket made out of silk and linen was actually worth it compared to the scratchy polyester one I had bought at Goodwill.

Nothing in the store jumped out at me. Literally. No black-robed wizards in training leaped out from behind a mannequin and invoked Cthulhu. Nothing else was strange. It seemed like an average, upscale consignment place. It would be nice to catch a break. At the rate I was going, I wouldn't have any back molars left to grind. I made another pass by a display of ironic T-shirts then headed back to the front.

The sales girl had been watching me closely. I wasn't used to such attention after years of neglect from the clerks at stores in New York. She was leaning on a jewelry display case filled with bracelets, necklaces, earrings, and rings.

Rings. I braved the rays of sunshine coming from her face and went over to look in the case. Most of the stuff was junk jewelry: pewter, fake gems, and a lot of big clunky rings like the one I had seen in Morty's bedroom. Sheila never used magic trinkets. I had never seen her wear rings or bracelets. The only piece she ever wore was a necklace I bought for her. She loved that one.

"Do you see something you like?"

"Why, yes." I pointed at the group of clunky ones. "I'm

quite interested in these rings. Can you tell me a little about them?"

"Beautiful, aren't they? Well, they're part of a set. They're supposed to be magical, if you believe in that kind of thing." She chuckled. "The gemstones indicate certain aspects or emotions that one would like to amplify. Red is for romance. Green is for wealth."

"Kind of like mood rings?"

"Oh, much better than that."

"How much are they?"

"I'm afraid they aren't for sale. They're display items. Our partner likes to keep them out to attract customers."

"What does purple stand for?"

"Purple is for creativity. Protection, mind strength, that sort of thing. But I don't think we have a purple one."

"I know. I recently came across one." I took Morty's ring out of my pocket.

The clerk's eyes widened. "Oh my! We recently had a theft, and that ring was stolen. We would very much like to have it back."

"I'll bet you would. I'm sure you promptly filed a police report."

Her eyes darted around. "Oh, of course."

"Sorry, but it was my friend's wish that I keep this for him."

"We could offer you a reward."

"Cut the crap."

"I'm sorry?"

"You heard me. This ring is not for sale. If your boss would like to meet with me, I might be willing to discuss returning it."

Her smile didn't waver. "I'm the owner of the shop. I don't have a boss."

"You mean your *partner* isn't the one in charge? It would mean absolutely nothing to you if I told you I needed to see Yareth?"

Her teeth were still showing, but I wouldn't have called her expression happy. "Not at all."

"Okay. Well, I'll be going. If Yareth, who you've never met, would like his ring back, tell him I'll be here at seven tomorrow morning." I headed out the door.

When I got back to the car, Orson was sitting in the passenger seat. *What happened?*

"I tried to stir things up. I'm not sure if it worked. Any trouble here?"

Some retirees were admiring the car, wondering if it was a V8.

"Were they suspicious?"

Blue shorts with black socks? You bet.

I scanned the area. I didn't spot a hit squad of goth rebels. Maybe Morty's mom just liked the scented candles at the New Age store. "You're sure about the shields?"

Yes.

I got in and sat behind the wheel.

What now?

I shook my head. "Good question."

TWELVE

I DECIDED IT WAS BEST TO watch the store and see if Yareth came by. I hoped he was the guy from the picture so I could recognize him. Of course, Orson insisted that I keep my promise first and buy his treats. So while I stared at the street, he chewed on a peanut butter doggie cookie shaped like Mickey Mouse ears.

Stakeouts always looked fun on TV. The two detectives would banter while they drank coffee, then the suspect strolled on up and did something incriminating. They would arrest the bad guy before the commercial break. No one got bored. No one had to go for a pee break.

Yareth must not have liked cop shows. Two hours had passed, but no one had gone in the clothing store, except a few college kids and a couple of tourists. None of them spent more than a few minutes inside, and no one carried bags when they left.

"You think Yareth has the day off?"

Maybe he went to Disney World. It's a small world after all. Orson whined the melody.

"Please don't sing."

Can we go to Disney World? You could get me a vest and pretend I'm a service dog.

Dogs.... Maybe we were at a dead end. Or perhaps Yareth only came by on Wednesdays and Saturdays. Maybe the coven back home was in on the whole thing, and they had tipped off Yareth, and he was staying away. I didn't know.

I had to keep the top up to make sure we weren't spotted, and the car was getting hot. I wiped sweat off my forehead with a questionable napkin I found in the cup holder. A two-hour wait to ride on Space Mountain was starting to seem more and more appealing.

A young woman of about twenty went into the store. She probably wanted something to wear back to school up north. I was about to recline my seat when she suddenly popped back out of the store, carrying a bag. Not only did she exit way too quickly, she was also the first person to buy anything all day. She hurried a few feet down the sidewalk and hopped into a Honda.

Suspicious, I started the car and followed her. I thought maybe Yareth had sent a minion.

Orson perked up. *Where we going?*

"I'll let you know when we get there."

She headed straight for the highway and got on going south. I stayed a few cars behind her. Fortunately, the college girl had a bright yellow Mean People Suck bumper sticker, which made her car easy to track. She didn't seem to be in any hurry. I was prepared for her to suddenly switch lanes or perform some other evasive maneuver in case she was being followed, but none of that happened. We were on the highway for about twenty-five minutes, getting caught in snarls around the theme park exits. She took the last Disney exit but drove away from the park and into a suburb apparently called Celebration based on the sign leading into it. I didn't know what it was with magic men and suburbs. I would have preferred to hide out in a proper lair, something with a moat.

Celebration looked like a prefab community that Disney had built to be the ideal all-American town, kind of like the Stepford Wives were supposed to be ideal all-American women. The neighborhood had lots of white picket fences, immaculate yards, and a Starbucks. I was pretty sure I shouldn't like Starbucks, but the frappuccinos were tasty.

The girl parked in front of a small colonial house not far from the main strip of restaurants and shops. I pulled over to the curb a few houses down. She hopped up the steps, and before she could even knock, the door opened. A fortyish man with a pointy goatee stood in the doorway.

He was the man from the picture. He took the bag from her and looked over her shoulder to check the street. I shrank back in my seat.

Is it him?

I hoped so. It was time to pay a visit. Once the girl in the Honda drove away, Orson and I could go over and—

"Hey, mister. Can I pet your dog?"

Orson and I jumped in our seats. A little tow-headed kid was standing outside the passenger side door, leaning toward the open window. He was dressed like he was heading to an *Andy Griffith Show* casting call.

"Well, can I?" He reached toward Orson with a sticky-looking hand.

"Uh... yeah. Sure. Just don't sneak up on him. He can be a little jumpy."

Opie eagerly rubbed Orson's head, while Orson whined nervously. I looked up in time to see the Honda rolling away from the house. Yareth had disappeared, too.

A security officer in an egg-shaped golf cart had pulled up on my side of the car. "Everything okay here, Timmy?"

"Hi, Officer Dan! I just wanted to pet the dog."

"Timmy, you know you shouldn't talk to strangers. You run along now." As the kid scampered off, Officer Dan glared at me. "And you shouldn't be talking to little boys." He scowled at me as if I were something he had scraped off his shoe. "You should get going, too."

"Really. That's how you treat tourists here?"

"For all I know, you pull this dog trick with kids up and down the coast. I could call for backup and run you through the system to see what comes up. Or you can just move along like I asked."

My blood boiled. I was about to say something about how I'd like to see him try when Orson whined and put his paw on my leg. There were bigger things at stake than fighting with a stupid rent-a-cop.

"Sure, Officer." I put the car in gear and drove away. "You got any plans tonight, Orson?"

I had planned a whole evening of scratching and chasing squirrels, but I can make time.

THIRTEEN

As much as I wanted to hang around and keep an eye on Yareth's house, it would have been too difficult to explain our situation to Celebration's version of Paul Blart. "No, I'm not trolling for kids! I'm just going to break into the house of an evil magician who may or may not be holding my witchy girlfriend hostage." Most people didn't react well when witches were mentioned.

When I met Sheila, she didn't tell me about the witch thing right away. I didn't blame her. She and I came from the same kind of background. The towns we grew up in weren't small, but they weren't exactly diverse, either. We were hardly a Bible Belt town, but any religion more exotic than Protestant or Catholic was looked on with a wary eye.

So after a couple of months of dating, Sheila sat me down on her couch and finally came out of the broom closet about being a witch. "It's a little hard to tell you this."

"It's okay. You know you can tell me anything."

"I know. It's just... this is very personal."

"Well, I know from experience that you aren't gay."

Sheila blushed. "Stop! This is important."

"Okay. Sorry."

"I'm... I'm a witch."

"You're a Wiccan? Oh, that's cool! I know all about Goddess Earth and that stuff." I had dated a college girl who was into Wicca while I was in basic training. She talked a lot about being in touch with the earth and female energies and chakras. I nodded a lot when she talked because she was cute.

Sheila glared at me. "*No.* Not a Wiccan. A witch."

"Isn't that what witches are called these days?"

"No. Wiccans are nice people who believe in nature gods and the power of women. Witches are... different." Sheila closed her eyes and breathed out her nose.

Orson padded over and hopped onto the couch to sit next to her. Her eyes opened, flashing gold. The door to the bedroom slammed shut, startling me. Then the bathroom door closed, followed by the open window and the door to the closet in the hall. I jumped with each slam, gaping as I stared around the room.

Sheila never took her eyes off me. "Yes. We're different."

That was my introduction to magic. Witches had power, although I was never exactly sure how much. I knew Sheila was special, but just how special was hard to say. She wasn't flashy about magic, but she did enough to impress the hell out of me. She was modest to a fault. It was hard enough to get her to talk about the magic stuff, but she was so self-effacing that she made it sound as if just about anyone could turn a pumpkin into a stagecoach.

I did find out a few things, some the hard way. I could never lie to her. She could always tell. I had gone to a friend's bachelor party and gotten home late. Sheila was waiting for me, and she asked if there had been any strippers there.

Being a little drunk, I said, "No! Of course not!"

She glared at me then stomped into the bedroom and shut the door. Orson trotted over, sat in front of the door, and growled at me any time I went near it. It took two days, a dozen roses, and a Big Mac before Orson grudgingly let me get close to her. That was a little unnerving.

Back at the hotel, I continued to think about that while

Orson nosed through a carton of takeout sesame chicken and brown rice with broccoli. White rice gave him gas. Well, so did broccoli, but the dog needed a balanced diet.

I wondered if Yareth really had magic. Sure, he could impress teenagers, but then so could a high score in *Call of Duty*. Making memories fuzzy couldn't be too high up on the list of things that needed magic. I had no idea how strong he was or if he was stronger than Sheila.

I shifted in the chair and felt something hard under me. I had forgotten about Morty's ring in my pocket. The store had been awfully interested in getting it back. Maybe it really did have magic, which would explain why they were a little obsessed.

I parted the curtains to get some light so I could examine the ring. The room had an excellent view of the suspiciously murky pool on the other side of the parking lot. A fat, hairy man lay facedown on a rusty lounge chair. He had been there when we pulled in, and I didn't think he had moved since then.

The purple stone picked up the light, and it gleamed but didn't sparkle. The clerk at the store had babbled something about how it amplified creativity and mind strength. Maybe it amplified things like Orson did.

I held up the ring. "What do you think of this?"

Orson gazed at it for a second. *It brings out your eyes. You trying to tell me something?*

"You're a big help. That clerk said these rings were magic. They had four others at the store and were very eager to complete the set with this one. Can you tell if it is magical?"

Orson padded over and sniffed at the ring. *I don't sense any power coming from it.* He stuck out his tongue and gave the stone a tiny lick. He reacted as if he had just stuck his tongue in an electrical socket, with his eyes popping wide and his fur standing up. *Whoa!* Orson started bouncing and leaping around the room. He hadn't moved like that since the time he lapped up some Red Bull I had spilled on the floor.

"Are you all right?"

Yeah. That was... wow! It's amazing!

"It's okay, pal. Walk it off. I think I get it."

The way Orson was acting made it clear that the ring acted as a booster. Those muscle heads in St. Augustine had said they couldn't remember Morty's face. It might have been the ring more than anything Goth Boy had done. Maybe we were on to something.

Wow! I can feel everything!

"Orson, come here!" I grabbed him by his scruff and slipped the ring onto his collar.

Hey! What are you doing?

"That ring is some kind of power amplifier."

I know.

"So why don't you use some of that power?"

What?

"Like, that powerful connection you have with Sheila."

Orson froze for a second then closed his eyes. Several minutes later, his eyes popped open. *I felt her!*

I picked him and stared at him. "Don't play with me."

I felt her. I did.

I hugged him close and fell onto the bed. A few tears rolled down my cheeks, then I dissolved in a full-on crying jag with big ragged sobs.

Orson licked my face. *I felt her. She's close!*

I let out a whoop. It was the first hint we had that Sheila was near and the first proof we had that she was still alive. *Hang on, Sheila. Your boys are coming.* "Where is she?"

I... I can't tell. He ducked his head, seeming embarrassed.

My joy diminished ever so slightly. "But you could feel her!"

Yes. She's hiding. The energy is odd, like a squirrel.

"A squirrel? What does that mean?"

He whined. *It's bouncing, elusive. It doesn't want to get caught.*

"How do you know she's close? How far away is she?"

She doesn't want to be found. It's only because I had that ring and that we're near that I could even feel her. But then she faded away.

"Could she feel you?"

I hope so. She's shielding herself. I tried to let her know we're here. I hope she heard me.

"Can you track her? Can you find her again?"

Orson closed his eyes and seemed to be concentrating hard. When he opened them again, he hung his head. *No. She's gone.*

I tried to hang on to my happy feelings, but they were slipping away. "Why would she hide from you like this?"

I don't know. But she is near.

Near. Celebration was near. We could be there in ten minutes. A big, bad magic man lived there, and he better have some answers for us. If he didn't, maybe that clerk would tell me more about the ring, if I asked extra nicely.

We waited until eleven to go back to Celebration so that it would be dark and the tourists wouldn't be out anymore. The night was quiet... well, Florida quiet, which meant I still heard the chirping of crickets and the droning of mosquitoes. Yareth's house was dark. I parked a block away, just in case any more golf-cart patrols decided to drive by. After one more look around, I climbed out of the car and headed to Yareth's house.

Orson trailed after me. *What's the plan?*

Either Yareth would tell me about the last time he'd seen Sheila or where she was, or I would use his head to remodel his house. I wasn't worried about spells. If Morty represented the level of power we were dealing with, then the whole thing would be over in two shakes of a gator's tail. "Kick his door down. Punch him in the face. Improvise after that."

Good plan. I like it.

As we got closer, we tried to keep an even pace and not sprint. A scowling man with a scurrying bulldog would probably be a bit conspicuous. A scowling man and a sauntering bulldog, that would blend in just fine.

I glanced at Orson. "Anything?"

Orson growled. *No. No shields. Not even an alarm.* He sniffed the air. *Smells familiar. Like that Morty kid.*

When we reached the front yard, I decided the better option would be a backdoor approach. We veered around the side and strolled into the backyard. I leapt up the porch steps and sent a kick to the door, just above the door knob. The cheap lock splintered noisily, the door swung open, and we stepped inside.

The house was empty. I could feel it. But I did a walk-through and checked anyway. There was no furniture, no food in the kitchen, no clothes, and no bed. Apparently, Yareth had been squatting there, or he just used the place as a front. He had cleared out in a hurry and left nothing behind, except an envelope taped to a wall in the living room. The envelope had my name on it.

I tore it down and ripped it open. A folded piece of paper and a necklace fell out. The necklace held a silver crescent moon. I had bought it for Sheila at a stand near the art museum after our second date.

I spun around to face Orson. "You said she was safe!"

She is! I could feel her.

"Then what is this?" I shoved the necklace in his face.

Orson whined and put his face in the carpet. Shaking my head, I opened the letter.

YOU HAVE SOMETHING I WANT. TIME TO TRADE.

At the bottom of the page was a stick-figure drawing of a dog. I crumpled the page and stuffed it into my pocket, along with Sheila's necklace.

FOURTEEN

I REVVED THE CAR AS WE sped down Vineland. I swerved around the few late-night drivers. They were all moving too slowly. Spending all day in amusement park lines and sticking around to watch the fireworks had obviously been exhausting. The minivan ahead of me slowed at a yellow light, and I had to slam the brakes to avoid hitting it.

"Is he telling the truth?"

Orson whined.

"You said she was hiding. You touched her!"

I did.

"Then how did he get the necklace?"

I don't know.

I cursed and hit the wheel. Orson was hunched down in the seat, paws over his nose.

"What the hell? How does that asshole get anywhere near Sheila? How does he get her necklace? And how do you not feel any of it?"

Stop.

"Don't tell me what to do! I've been counting on you, and it's gotten us nowhere."

Stop.

"I will not stop! We've been at this for days, and we're still chasing shadows and magic bullshit and—"

Orson barked, the anger and sorrow radiating off of him so strong it was like a fist to my chest. *Stop!*

I shut up. The car behind me honked, snapping me back

to attention. The light had turned green. After another block, I peeked at Orson. He was slumped back down in the seat, looking desolate. It had to have been worse for him. He had actually touched her.

"I'm sorry."

Orson didn't answer.

"Come on. You got my hopes up. I'm sorry. We've got to regroup and see what we can do."

I pulled into the parking lot of our crappy motel. The fat, hairy man was no longer by the pool. Either he had been kicked out by the hotel staff for being at the pool after hours or the morgue truck had finally retrieved him.

Back in the motel room, Orson walked over and curled up in a corner, facing the wall. He whined softly, while I tried to think. Sheila was still nearby. Orson knew she was close. But I had no idea where. Morty and that meathead in St. Augustine had said Orson was the key to the whole fiasco, but I couldn't figure out why Yareth would want Orson.

I couldn't focus. The moldy walls were making me claustrophobic. So was the guilt I was feeling about yelling at poor Orson. I needed a break. "Orson, I'm going to get coffee. Do you want to come?"

When Orson didn't answer, I sighed and went out into the muggy air. I trudged to the next-door—ironically twenty-four-hour—7-Eleven, where the coffee was at least drinkable. I picked up some gummi bears for me and some Slim Jims to make nice with Orson.

Leaning against the outside wall of the store, I sipped my coffee, which was quickly becoming lukewarm. Either that or I was so out of it that I didn't realize how much time was passing. I shouldn't have yelled at Orson, but I was getting so frustrated. No one wanted to give me a straight answer about anything.

I tried to think about what to do next. Maybe I should show up at the store when it opened and see if Yareth was there. He certainly wasn't going back to the house in Celebration. *Maybe I should drop Orson off at the shop with a bow around his collar and see what happens.* That seemed like a dumb idea, unlike all the brilliant ones I'd had so far.

A car with Mississippi plates pulled up to one of the gas pumps out front. A wobbly teen lurched out from behind the wheel and pulled the nozzle from its holder. He opened his gas tank but had trouble finding the hole.

The girl in the passenger seat cackled. "C'mon, Jason! Stick it in there!"

"Yeah, I'll stick it in!"

"If you can find it!"

They both howled.

I had an idea. Maybe it would let me know how much the coven wasn't telling me. Maybe I could get Yareth going in the wrong direction. I strolled over to the gas pump. "Hey, how's it going?"

"Never better!"

I could smell about twelve Coors Lights on his breath. "I see that. You want me to call you a cab?"

"Fuck that! I'm doing great." After a few more tries, he finally got the nozzle in the gas tank.

"Right. Do you mind if I use your phone to call one for me? My battery died." I held up five bucks.

"Shit man, whatever." He lobbed his phone at me, and I gave him the money. "The lockout code is 6969."

Of course it was. "Thanks, pal. You're a life saver." I went back over to the store wall and leaned against it while I dialed a New York number. It was one in the morning. I hoped I would be waking her up.

"Hello?" She sounded super groggy and confused.

Good. "Hi, Lisa. It's me."

"Gabriel? Do you know what time it is?"

"Time for you to stop fucking around."

"What?"

"Yareth was waiting for us. It was a setup."

"What?" Her voice became clearer. "Are you okay?"

"No thanks to you. You're the only person I told I was coming here. So who do you think told Yareth?"

"I didn't! I've been trying to help."

"Sure, by pointing me straight to him. I've been following the trail you left for me. So what's the deal? Are you working with this asshole?"

"I don't know what you're talking about. I never heard the name until you said it to me the other day."

I wanted to slam the phone onto the ground. "Sheila always liked you. You were her friend! Did you set up the disappearance, too?"

"I would never hurt her. She helped me get away from David when he was hurting me. Why would you think...?" She began to cry.

Great. Maybe she was being honest. From what Sheila had told me, David got off on hurting Lisa. He sounded like someone I used to know. And David had been hard to get rid of. He kept trying to stop Lisa from moving out. He would show up unannounced and threaten her. It took a good deal of magical persuasion from Sheila, along with a restraining order, to get him to go away.

Still, there were too many coincidences to explain. "Lisa, listen. She wasn't in Florida. I'm in Mississippi now."

"Why are you there? Didn't you have a good lead on her?"

"Yareth let slip something about a camp he had up near Gulfport. It's all I've got right now." Maybe that would throw them off the trail a bit. I downed the last of my cold coffee. "I gotta go. I'll call if I find anything else." I hung up.

A squeal of tires behind me made me jump. The drunk teens had weaved off. He'd forgotten about his cell phone. *Oh goody.* I could play *Angry Birds* again.

I chucked the coffee cup into a trashcan and headed back to our resort accommodations. The lot was dark except for a dim light from the one working lamppost and the glow from an open door.

My door. Which I knew I had locked.

FIFTEEN

STUPID, STUPID, STUPID. THEY HAD said I was unimportant and they wanted Orson. So of course I had to get in a fight and leave him alone. I told myself to calm down and think.

Orson hadn't yelped, either out loud or in my head. He was probably fine. Maybe I hadn't shut the door all the way, and it just blew open. I jogged across the lot, aiming for the left side of the door. I pressed my body against the wall between the doorway and the window. I didn't hear anything except the TV. Then, something shuffled across the carpet.

I set down the bag of snacks and dug into my pocket for my blackjack. Leaning over, I peered into the room.

A woman with curly blond hair was standing over the bed and rummaging through my duffle bag. She was the clerk from the consignment store. She was probably still smiling. Orson was nowhere to be seen.

I couldn't hurt her too badly until I found out what had happened to Orson. Also, I'd seen my mom bruised up enough that I never wanted to ever hit any woman. I crept up behind her, hoping she wouldn't hear me, so I could toss her onto the bed.

The drunk teen's phone in my pocket farted. I wasn't surprised that the jackass had fart sounds for his ring tone, but I still jumped. He was probably calling because he realized that he'd forgotten to get his phone back.

Store Lady spun around, and I glimpsed a flash of something metallic in her hand. I smacked her hand on pure reflex and pushed her onto the bed. She had a little pink gun. With a decal or two, it could have been a Hello Kitty souvenir for pre-teens.

I snatched the gun and kept it trained on her as I walked over to close the door. "What are you doing here?" I checked the gun and made sure it was loaded. I didn't look to see if the bullets were pink.

She shook her head. "You know why. You have something that belongs to us."

I hauled her off the bed with one hand and jammed the gun under her chin. "What did you do with him?"

"Aah!" Her eyes widened. "Who?"

"Don't play dumb. You know what I mean."

"No, I—"

"You've got till three. Then we'll see what your toy gun can do."

"Wait."

"One."

"I don't know—"

"Two." I ground the gun in harder.

"No, don't—"

"Three."

She screamed. "I don't know what you're talking about!"

I eased the gun back a bit. "One last time. Where is the dog?"

She looked genuinely surprised. "Dog? What dog?"

"The dog that was in this room when you came in!" I jammed the gun back in her neck. "You'd better tell me."

She gasped. "I don't know anything about the dog. I just came here to get the ring."

I dropped her back on the bed. She grunted, and the cheap springs squeaked loudly.

"How did you get in?" I asked her.

"I told the front desk I was your girlfriend and that

78

I was here to surprise you. Well, and I gave her twenty dollars."

I made a mental note: no check-out tip for her. "What about the dog? He wouldn't let you in."

"I told you, there was no dog."

I was stunned, but it had to be true. If Orson had been there, she would never have gotten into the room. I pulled the cord off the lamp and used it to tie the clerk to the chair. I didn't trust her to sit still while I searched the room. I checked in the bathroom and under the bed. I didn't find any claw marks or blood.

I sat on the bed and studied the wayward clothing clerk. "What's your name?"

"How dare you? You don't know what you're doing."

I shrugged and picked up her purse. Her license said she was Kathryn Morrison. And her address was very familiar. She was Morty's mom. "So how's Morty doing?"

She sputtered, and her eyes bugged out a little. "What?"

"Little Morty, or does he go by Malvolio now?"

She sighed. "I told him that was a stupid name. But did he listen? No. Whatever Yareth tells him..."

"No offense, but he's not the sharpest wand in the sharp wand holder."

She shook her head. "Don't get me started."

At least it seemed Mommy Dearest was getting into a more talkative mood. "So all that stuff today about not knowing who Yareth was, that was crap."

"Yeah."

"Do you know where he is?"

"No. I've barely seen him all month. Morty brought him to the store last month, and he comes by now and then. My boy doesn't have a lot of friends, so I was glad to see him with someone. But now that guy has Morty running errands for him day and night. He barely comes home anymore."

"What's up with the rings?"

"I really don't know. Yareth uses my store as a hub for his followers. He put the rings out as a signal that the store is 'protected.' He said they were magic, but really, who believes in that? I mean, my ex took me to Siegfried and Roy on our honeymoon and all. The tigers were cool, but magic?"

I didn't say anything. Orson had sensed shields, and the ring really was magical, so there must have been something to it.

"Anyway, one of the rings went missing last week. Yareth was really mad about it, accusing his 'enemies' of plotting against him. So when you came by and flashed it around, I told him about it. Yareth told me to come and get it tonight. He called me an hour ago and told me where you were staying and that I should get it while you were out. I saw you at the gas station when I drove in."

"And there wasn't a dog here?"

She shook her head. "No, I already told you."

Still, there was no Orson. The only traces of him were some scraps of sesame chicken and the fancy dog cookies I had left for him, the Donald Duck one, the big sun, the palm tree—

Wait. I hadn't gotten him a palm tree cookie. Only two bites had been taken out of it. Orson would eat coffee grounds, so it was hard to believe the treat had tasted too bad to finish. I picked up the cookie and saw some white powder residue around one bite mark. Flipping it over, I found that someone had jammed a couple of pills into it.

I turned back to the woman. "Yareth told you where I was?"

"Yes."

"You didn't follow me?"

She shook her head. "No. The store doesn't close until eight. I can't leave it to go traipsing around Florida because some weirdo Morty hangs out with tells me to."

That college kid I followed to Yareth's house must have

been a setup. She had led me right to Yareth and the fake hideout so I could then be tailed, and I had been too keyed up to notice. And when Orson and I went back to Yareth's, the girl had probably snuck into the room and mixed those drugged doggie snacks in with the ones I'd bought for him. The motel key-card locks were hardly foolproof. All the girl would have had to do was swipe the master off a maid cart.

"I followed a college kid down here. About twenty, long brown hair. You know her?"

"That was probably Madison. She works for me on the weekends."

"You know where she lives?"

"Yeah, but what do you want with her?"

I went over and untied her. "Get up. We're going out."

SIXTEEN

I MADE KATHRYN GET IN ON the driver's side and slide over into the passenger seat so I could keep the gun on her. I wouldn't have shot her—well, I was pretty sure I wouldn't—but she didn't know that.

I got behind the wheel and poked her with the gun. "Show me how to get to Madison's. And don't try any funny business."

She nodded nervously. "Go left at the next light."

As I drove, I desperately searched my mind for any hint of Orson. Nothing. I couldn't hear his voice. I was so used to Orson being in the background that the silence was frightening.

The first time Orson "spoke" to me, I thought I was imagining it. Sheila was out of town on an expedition for the store, and I was watching the Mets destroy the hopes and dreams of all their fans. They were up by one run in the ninth, but the free-agent closer they'd spent twenty million on had just walked three batters in a row. Then the guy proceeded to serve up a meatball that Chipper Jones smacked into the parking lot of Turner Field. The Braves mobbed the future Hall of Famer at home plate. The Mets pitcher just shrugged as he left the field.

I reacted calmly and maturely by flinging the remote control into the wall. It shattered and caused Orson to jump up from his nap.

Hey!

It sounded as if someone was standing behind me, but there was no one else in the apartment. The window was open, so I decided it must have been someone on the street or upstairs. Orson was sitting up on his pillow and whining.

I went over to scratch his head. "Sorry, boy. Did I wake you?"

Orson whined and grunted at me. *Yeah. You did.*

I gasped and fell back onto the couch. "Wha—"

Your tantrum woke me up. I'm telling Mama.

"Wha—"

I can see why Mama loves you. Such conversation.

"Sorry. Remote... the Mets..."

Don't blame them. I'm a dog, and I know they're terrible.

A dog was talking to me, and all I could do was blame the Mets for breaking the remote. "How... how are you doing that?"

Oh. Right. Woof. Bow-wow, duh, bow-wow. He promptly went back to sleep on his pillow, or at least he closed his eyes and pretended to sleep.

I was worried I was going crazy. But two weeks before that, I hadn't believed in magic, either.

When Sheila got back that night, I eased into the topic by first asking, "How was your trip?"

She kissed me and brushed a strand of hair from in front of her beautiful green eyes. "Oh, you know. I had to find some exotic mystical treasures to keep the forces of darkness at bay. How was your weekend?"

"Oh, fine. Mostly hung out. Uh, by the way, does Orson ever...?"

"What? Did something happen to Orson? Is he okay?"

"He's fine. He's on his bed. But... ah... does he ever, um, talk?"

Sheila gave me a funny look. "Well, he can bark in a way that sounds like he's saying 'Mama' or sometimes 'I love you.' Why?"

"Oh, nothing. I just, um, I heard him... talk to me. I woke him up, and he complained about it."

Sheila just stared at me as if I were describing some flying pink elephants I'd seen. "How many beers did you have?"

"I had two all weekend. I did not imagine it."

"Okay. I think I'm going to go lie down and unpack." She headed into the bedroom.

Orson, who was supposedly asleep, hopped up and trotted after her. She closed the door behind them. I sat and watched TV. Maybe I was crazy. The Mets could do that to a guy.

The next morning, Sheila went out to the store to deliver whatever she'd brought back for the coven. Orson stared at me while I sipped my coffee.

"Well, thanks, pal. Now Sheila thinks I'm crazy."

Not my fault.

I spewed coffee all over the table. Orson barked gleefully.

"Stop it! You are not talking. Dogs don't talk."

Okay. I'm not talking. It's all a dream. Oooooo...

I sat there, not knowing how to respond to that.

Fortunately, Orson was feeling chatty. *It's part of the familiar thing. We can talk to each other.*

"I'm not a witch."

Duh. But you're part of our pack now.

"The coven hates me. They basically threw me out of their Christmas party."

Solstice party. And you even brought chili. But it's not the coven. Our *pack. She loves you. You make her happy. That means I love you, too.*

My eyes watered a little. It had been a long time since I'd felt as though I was a part of anything, let alone a family. But hearing it from a dog was still weird. "Can you do this with anyone?"

No. Just the pack.

"How long have you been able to do this?"

With her, forever. With you, not too long.

"Why didn't she tell me?"

She was going to tell you at your anniversary dinner, but your little outburst surprised me, and I let it slip out.

"Sorry. Was she mad about the remote?" Sheila had worked so hard to help me rein in my temper. Her disappointed expression when I screwed up was heartbreaking.

Didn't tell her. I told her I fell asleep under the couch and you stepped on my tail.

Man's best friend covering for me already. "Thanks, buddy."

She loves you. Don't ever hurt her.

"Don't worry. I love her, too."

We know.

Sheila came back that afternoon and found Orson lying on my lap. He had rolled over so I could rub his belly.

"Did you two have a nice chat?" She winked at me.

I never actually came out and asked her if she had long talks with Orson. She never asked me, either. She did like to make the occasional joke about me being crazy.

I sometimes wondered if I really was crazy for talking to a dog and hearing the dog talk back. But Sheila would nudge Orson, then she would giggle and Orson would chuff like he was laughing.

But Orson wasn't speaking to me in that motel room. And the silence was overwhelming.

SEVENTEEN

KATHRYN DIRECTED ME TO DRIVE into downtown Orlando and turn east on Colonial. Heading away from the bright lights and into the more run-down area of town, with cracked sidewalks, shuttered storefronts, and broken streetlights, I kept one hand on the wheel and the other on the little pink gun in my pocket. I had untied her because a woman with her hands tied in a convertible would probably attract police attention.

"Straight ahead, just past the movie theater." She pointed at a strip mall dominated by a decrepit theater. The sign promised "All Seats $2!" The movies were all at least two months old. "Take the next left."

She fumed in the seat next to me. I wasn't thrilled about her being there, either, but I wasn't about to cut her loose. She didn't seem to be exactly enthralled by Yareth, but I couldn't take any chances. She was probably only going along with me to make sure her son was safe. If she knew how I'd left him... well, it was a good thing I had the gun.

"Where did you get that ring?" she asked.

"Found it."

"Oh really? When did you see my son?"

"About two days ago."

Her eyes widened. "Where is he?"

Running away from alligators on the Florida coast. "I don't know."

"Did he give you that ring?"

"No."

"He has keys to the shop. I had a feeling he stole it. Yareth made such a big deal about those rings. I was sure Morty stole it so he could be powerful, like his idol." She sighed.

"That didn't work so good."

She gave me a puzzled look. "Why do you want Yareth?"

"Don't fuck with me."

"I let Morty's friends hang out in the storeroom, but what they talk about is their business."

"My girlfriend disappeared two weeks ago. I've tracked her down here, and Mortimer was the last one to see her, as far as I know."

I really hated using the term "girlfriend" to refer to Sheila. As far as I was concerned, no one out of high school should be allowed to use that word for their significant other. Sometimes Sheila jokingly called me her "lover." I once tried calling her "my woman," but I didn't like the eye rolls she gave me. I sometimes wondered why I wasn't calling her "fiancée" or "wife."

Kathryn gasped. "You think he's involved in kidnapping your girlfriend?"

"He admitted it."

"I never thought they'd get that far." Her voice wavered. "They just seemed to like hanging out and listening to bad music. Yareth likes to talk, but I never took him seriously." She pointed. "Over there, on the right."

I pulled up to the shabby apartment building she'd indicated. It seemed to be sagging in the middle. The two stories held four apartments, and the two upper ones had their own stairways to the street. Parked in front was the Honda with the bumper sticker, the same car I had followed that afternoon.

She folded her arms. "Maddy's in 2A. On the left."

I reached for the door handle. "Great. Let's go."

"What?"

"You think I'm leaving you in the car? Move."

I climbed out and held the door open as she slid over the console and exited the car. I walked behind her as she crossed the lot, entered the building, and moved up the stairs. I nudged her with the gun whenever she hesitated to make sure she didn't try anything stupid.

When we reached the top, I nudged Kathryn toward the door then put the gun in my pocket. "Don't do anything stupid, just get her to open the door." The last thing I needed was to have one of them get the bright idea of jumping me and the gun go off accidentally.

Kathryn nodded. I pushed her in front of the peephole and banged on the door. I slid to the side, out of view. On the other side, someone shuffled to the door. I gestured at Kathryn.

"Madison?" Kathryn called. "It's me. Open up!"

"Kathryn? Do you know what time it is?"

"I'm sorry, but this is important."

The door opened a crack, but the woman kept the chain on the door. "Can't this wait until—"

I leapt forward, slamming all my weight into the door. The cheap chain popped free, and the door swung open. Madison cried out as she got knocked into the wall. I pulled Kathryn in behind me and shut the door.

I grinned. "Hello, Madison."

Madison rubbed the bump on her head as she looked up at me. Her eyes widened with recognition. "You! What are you doing here?"

"I want my dog."

Madison tilted her head smugly and regained her composure. "I don't know what you're talking about."

I craned my neck to check out the small apartment. The small entryway led to a large room with a kitchen area at one end. An open door on the far wall showed a tiny bathroom with a shower stall. Everything was sparse and neat. I didn't see a bag of dog food or anything else that might indicate Orson had been there. Some jackets hung on hooks by the door. Sticking out of the pocket of one was a curly yellow piece of elastic attached to a clip. I'd seen those elastics clipped to hotel maids. I tugged on the elastic, and a hotel card key with a castle printed on it popped out of the pocket.

I held up the card. "Really? You didn't happen to be at the Kingdom of Magic and just happen to pick up a master key card?"

"That's from last week when some friends came to town. They stayed there."

"You put them up in that dump, and they're still your friends? I saw you today. You led me right to Celebration."

"So? I didn't take your stupid bulldog."

I punched the wall beside her head, leaving a hole in the cheap drywall. Madison shrieked and ducked, covering her head with her arms. Kathryn flinched and edged back toward the door. I glared at Kathryn and shook my head.

I sent Sheila a mental apology for getting angry. I pointed at Madison. "If you didn't see him, how did you know he's a bulldog?"

"Because Yareth told us you were bringing him."

"When did he tell you that?"

"About two weeks ago."

That was about the time I had started asking the coven questions about Sheila. They knew. Those witches were in on it.

My punch had knocked some mail off a small side table by the wall. On the floor next to the envelopes was a wax paper bag with a logo from The Bark-ery. I picked up the bag and opened it to find more of the palm tree cookies I'd found in the room. I punched the wall on her other side. "You've got about one minute to tell me where I can find Yareth and where I can find my dog."

"I don't know where—"

I pulled my fist back. "I'm running out of wall."

Kathryn grabbed my arm. "Stop! She's just a kid!"

Things were getting bad. I was losing control. I didn't want to hurt them. My anger was getting the better of me, and my actions were making me a little queasy. But I needed Orson back, and I need to find Sheila, and they were my only leads.

Kathryn was scared; mostly of me, I guessed. But kidnapping dogs and girlfriends was a lot more than she'd signed up for, not to mention me having to threaten people right in front of her. Maybe I could work that. "These people screwed with your son, took over your shop, and made you break into hotels. And now you're actually defending them?"

"I can't let you hurt her."

"It's not up to you." I jabbed a finger at Madison. "It's all on her."

The trembling Madison tried to take a step back, but she was up against the wall. "Yareth said you'd be like this. He knew you'd try to threaten me. He knew. You are not fit to care for that creature. But it's fine." She reached into her pocket. "He knows I would never betray him."

Madison pulled her hand out of her pocket. Expecting a weapon, I reached into my pocket with my free hand, ready to pull out the gun. Instead, she held up a bottle. She quickly unscrewed the cap and tilted the bottle so the contents flowed into her mouth.

I tried to step forward, but Kathryn was still holding my arm. "What the hell? Stop!"

"I will never betray him. And you will not find them." She stumbled back then slid down the wall to sit on the floor.

Kathryn let go of me and moved to kneel beside the woman. "Madison, what did you do? Are you okay?"

Madison gave her a groggy-looking smile. "I was brave. Yareth will be happy." Her eyes fluttered shut.

Kathryn put her hand under the woman's nose then looked up at me. "She's breathing."

I knelt on the other side of Madison and put my hands on her shoulders. "Hey! Wake up!" I shook her a little.

Kathryn placed her hand on mine. "That's not going to help. I don't know what was in that bottle, but it knocked her out cold."

EIGHTEEN

"**D**AMN IT!" I CLENCHED MY fist and ground my teeth. I wanted to smash everything in her apartment, but that wouldn't do anything except bruise my knuckles. I called 9-1-1 from Madison's phone, then I dragged Kathryn toward the door.

"Is she going to be all right?" Kathryn asked. "I really should stay with her."

I pulled her out into the hallway. "No, we're leaving."

"But—"

"The paramedics will help her." I continued dragging Kathryn down the stairs. Back at the car, I opened the driver's side door and gestured. "You know the drill. Get in."

She climbed in and slid over into the passenger seat. After scanning the lot, I got behind the wheel. I had no desire to explain what had happened or why I was there with a woman I barely knew. *No, really, Officer. I was only threatening this girl because she kidnapped my talking dog. She drugged herself to get away from me.* I slapped the wheel. I should have been smarter. I was getting sloppy because I was freaking out about Sheila and Orson. And I was running out of leads. I backed out of the lot then turned toward downtown.

"Can I go home now?" Kathryn sounded tired.

I still didn't know how much I could trust her, but her question gave me an idea. "No, but you'll *feel* at home."

Fifteen minutes later, I parked in front of her store. That place was my last resort for getting a clue to where Yareth was.

"What are we doing?" she asked.

"You're going to let me in. I want to see the back room where your son and his band of geeks hang out."

"Why?"

I patted my pocket that held the gun. "Because I asked." I hated having to use the poor women. And unlike some of my military buddies, I had never been a fan of guns. Sheila would have known that, but I was glad the woman didn't. "Don't do anything stupid, and you'll be just fine."

I waited for her nod of agreement before opening my door. Climbing out, I stayed bent over so I could keep an eye on her. I wasn't sure what I would do if she popped open the passenger door and made a run for it. Fortunately, that didn't seem to occur to her. She slid over, got out, and followed me up to the door.

I gestured at the lock. "Come on. I don't have all night."

Scowling, she unlocked the door then turned to the wall beside it to shut off the alarm. I watched her carefully, but I realized she might enter a special code that would get the police on their way. I couldn't afford to linger.

I hustled over to the display case. The rings, except for the purple one, were still there. That was good. Since they were magic, Yareth would have taken them with him if he was planning to leave town. I turned back to Kathryn. "Now, take me to little Morty's playroom."

She led me down the aisle, past the torn jeans and vintage T-shirts, and to a black curtain. I stepped in front of her and ripped the curtain aside. Kathryn gasped. Apparently, she hadn't been back there recently. The walls were covered in jet-black velvet. Intricate candelabras stood on almost every horizontal surface. But the focus of the tableau was the black throne in the center of the room. Pentacles were inlaid into the back, and skulls were carved on the handrests.

Kathryn covered her mouth. "Oh, Morty. What are you doing?"

I glanced at her. "You really had no idea?"

"No! You think I would let them do"—she waved her hand at the room—"this to my storeroom?"

"You said they were here a month. You must have come in here to get something."

"I did. All the time. But I-I don't remember any of this being here. He couldn't have put all of this in here today, could he? Why didn't I see it?"

I believed her. Morty hadn't even been able to remember the location of the lair, and it was in the back of his mom's store. Yareth could certainly make people forget things he didn't want them to know.

Madison had only had a few minutes' head start. If she had snuck in just ahead of Kathryn, she couldn't have gone too far, especially if she had to ditch Orson before she went back to her apartment. It had taken us fifteen minutes to go from her place to here.

"When you came back here, where did you get your stock?"

"Um... I thought it was right here." She gestured around the room. "But I guess not."

"But you had back stock, right? I mean you came out of the room with jeans and shirts and whatever?"

Kathryn looked as though she wasn't sure that gravity would still work if she took a step forward. "I... um, I think so. I must have. Right?"

"Come on. Think! Is there a basement or another room back here?"

She shook her head, and her eyes started to glisten with tears. "I can't remember! Why can't I remember?"

Great. Whatever block Yareth had given her was working overtime.

I walked to the right and began knocking at various places on the wall. The velvet didn't give until I passed the corner and started on the next wall. There, the fabric was stretched across an open space. I looked up and saw that the material was stapled to the ceiling.

Giving the curtain a hard yank, I tore it away to reveal some stacks of boxes and clothing racks. I began picking up boxes and throwing them out into the main room. Kathryn, seeming to be in shock, just stood there and stared around the room. She almost got hit by a box, but she didn't even flinch.

I slumped back. Orson wasn't there. I'd lost him. I'd lost Sheila. It was all gone.

And then I smelled something. Sesame chicken.

Orson always farted in his sleep. Whatever shields or blocks Yareth had put around Orson couldn't hold that odor.

I moved the last clothing rack away from the wall. The long dresses had been hiding a small box. When I pulled it toward me, the box shifted as though something inside had rolled over. I opened the lid.

Orson lay on his back, snoring and farting.

"Pepe Le Pew had nothing on you, my man." I picked him up and hugged him hard enough to make the stench worse.

His awful breath was on my cheek, hot and shallow. He didn't wake up. *Come on, Orson. Be okay.* I carried him out of the store room.

Kathryn had sunk to the floor. She looked up as I passed. "Oh. You found him."

Ignoring her, I continued out into the store. I stopped at the jewelry case. With Kathryn's gun, I smashed the glass and scooped up the rings. They were heavier than they looked. I left the pink gun in their place. I hurried out to the car and carefully laid Orson in the passenger seat.

I got on the turnpike, heading north. I kept blinking and zoning out as the adrenaline wore off. Once, I almost drifted into the next lane, but a honk from the car behind me jolted me awake.

I didn't know where I was going. I certainly didn't want to go back to the hotel. I could just imagine hordes of Yareth followers lying in wait there. We hadn't left anything in the room that I couldn't replace.

After about thirty miles, I pulled into a rest area. It was close to four in the morning, and I was exhausted. I figured I would take a quick nap before continuing. I put the top up on the car then closed my eyes.

NINETEEN

I OPENED MY EYES TO BLINDING sunlight. My watch said it was nine o'clock. Orson whimpered and waved his paw around, scratching at his head.

I rubbed his belly. "Orson! Come on. Wake up."

He let out a low moan and opened his eyes. *What the hell?*

"Orson! You're okay!" I reached out and scratched his head.

Quiet. Ow! That hurts. He tried to stand. *Oh. Let me...*

"What?"

Let me out! Out!

I leaned over him and opened the door. Orson rolled out and landed with a thump. He staggered to his feet and proceeded to puke all over the asphalt. I jumped out and ran around the car. Fortunately, we were alone in our section of the parking lot so I didn't have to worry about him getting run over.

"It's okay. You're going to be okay."

When he was finally done, I lifted him back into the car. "I'll be right back, Orson."

I ran into the rest stop and got a bottle of water and a roll from the coffee shop. I poured the water into a cup. He eagerly lapped it up then nibbled warily at the roll.

"Do you remember anything?"

Not much. You left, and I ate some of the cookies you

bought me. I got sleepy and nodded off. I remember a woman picked me up. I think I remember going out a window.

"That's all?"

Yeah.

I filled him in on the adventures of the past evening. About Mama Morty and the lair in her storeroom and Madison, the devoted servant.

What do you think they were going to do with me?

"Well, if they have Sheila, I'm guessing they were going to take you to her. Then, they would force her to make you do... whatever."

I guess. But they don't have her.

"I have a necklace that says otherwise."

I don't know how they got her necklace. But I'm sure they don't have her.

"Because of that ring?"

Orson nodded.

"You don't think the ring could have been a trick?"

He stared at me. *He'd have to be more powerful than Sheila to pull that off.*

"I don't know how powerful she really is. I don't know many witches. Or wizards, for that matter."

She's strong.

"Well, after meeting Morty, I was ready to write Yareth off as a joke. But I just watched a girl risk killing herself rather than give him up or tell me where you were."

That comet cult guy got people to kill themselves. He wasn't magic. Just crazy.

"Good point. But I still don't think we should underestimate them. I did that yesterday, and I almost lost you."

Orson suddenly became very interested in the roll he had only nibbled at.

"Orson, I'm sorry about last night. I was just frustrated. I shouldn't have left you alone."

You owe me some taquitos.

I carefully rubbed his head. I noticed the ring was still

on his collar. Maybe Madison had left it on to keep tabs on him. Yareth had found us pretty quickly. "How's the ring doing?"

I forgot it was on.

I slipped the ring off his collar. "Feel any different?"

Orson shook his head a bit. *Can't tell. I'm still pretty foggy.* Until he got back to normal, it would be hard to judge the true power of the rings.

"I'm thinking that might be how they tracked us down."

And you just took four more of them. For a drugged-up dog, he was making a lot of sense. I was tempted to pitch them all into the trash, but that purple ring was the only thing that had gotten us close to Sheila. I would risk getting tailed for that reward.

"I need coffee. Can I leave you alone without you getting kidnapped again?"

We'll see.

I ran back into the store and grabbed a cup of coffee and an egg sandwich. Hurrying back outside, I scanned the parking lot. It was still empty. Orson was lying on the passenger seat, chewing on the roll. I sipped my coffee.

I couldn't imagine why on earth some cult leader wanted Orson so badly. I needed to talk to someone. I couldn't trust anyone at the coven, including—maybe especially—Lisa. "So, you know of any covens in Florida?"

Oh sure. I think they have a pavilion at Epcot.

"You're a big help."

An electronic fart broke the silence. I had forgotten that stupid phone. I pulled it out of my pocket and read the text message: *DUDE GIVE ME MY PHONE BACK!!!!!*

I ignored the text, but I suddenly got an idea. I did a quick Google search then cranked the engine.

Where are we going?

"Lakeland. We should be there in ninety minutes."

Why?

"They have a good sandwich place there."

TWENTY

U NTIL THAT MORNING, ALL I had known about Lakeland was that it was the home of Tiger Town. One of my army friends was from Detroit and a huge Tigers fan. He used to talk about retiring down in Lakeland and watching his team in spring training.

When I Googled "Central Florida Witch," I found an article in the Orlando Sentinel about a Lakeland Community College teacher who was suing the school for wrongful dismissal. She was a comparative religion professor, but the school found out that she was a Wiccan and suggested that maybe she shouldn't be quite so comparative.

In the article, she corrected the reporter. He asked her to comment on her being a Wiccan, and she replied, "No, dear, I'm not Wiccan. I'm a witch." That was exactly how Sheila had phrased it. The article had also mentioned that, since her dismissal, she was working at the sub shop she had inherited from her father. She had renamed the restaurant the Sand Witch.

Visiting the woman was a long shot, but it was better than trying to tangle with Yareth again.

I pulled up outside the Sand Witch. The sign had a busty cartoon girl wearing a 1920s bathing suit and riding a broom. Blond curls poked out from under her pointy black hat. We waited in the car for a few minutes to scope out the street. I didn't see anything suspicious.

There were no customers inside the place, so I figured it would be a good time to go in and ask questions.

Orson trundled along next to me as I walked up the path to the door. *Do you think she knows Yareth?*

I shrugged.

Do you think she works with him?

"I don't know, but I don't know what else to do. You'll have to be alert." Orson seemed a bit groggy. "How are you doing?"

Better.

"You feel anything?"

There's something here. That's for sure. It's different. It doesn't feel like the store did. Or Yareth's house.

Under the circumstances, "different" was great. Maybe we weren't wasting our time after all. "Okay, let's go. Make sure you aren't noticed until we can check it out."

Apparently too tired to talk back, he just rolled his eyes at me.

A bell rang as we entered. There was a plump lady behind the counter with her back to us, slicing up tomatoes.

"I'm sorry. Animals aren't allowed inside. Even cute ones."

I stopped in my tracks. There weren't any mirrors in the room.

Orson shook his head. *I don't know either.*

"Oh, you can tell him that those tricks don't work in here. Not while I'm around." She turned to face us. She had a smile on her round face. "I'd ask you what you'd like to eat, but I have a feeling you're not here for the food."

I can always eat. I could go for some salami.

"Aren't you the little heartbreaker? We have the best in Central Florida." She took a piece of meat from the counter and tossed it to him.

Orson caught it on the air and snarfed it up. His love of spiced meat covered up any surprise he may have felt at the fact that she had responded to him.

I was pretty sure my shock showed on my face, though. "Did you *hear* him?"

"Of course, dear."

I frowned. "But I—"

"You shouldn't do that! It gives you little lines on your forehead."

It's okay. She's one of us.

I looked between the two of them. Orson seemed way too calm.

The lady chuckled. "He means witches. Magical creatures. People sensitive to that world." She gestured toward a booth. "Why don't you have a seat?"

I was too tired and overwhelmed to protest. I walked over and slid into the booth. I did make sure to choose the side facing the door.

She scooted around the counter, walked over, and locked the door. She flipped the window sign over to Closed. "Now, let me get you some coffee, and you can tell me what's on your mind."

"Light cream. No sugar."

She brought over a steaming cup of coffee and placed it in front of me. "Here you are." She slid into the seat across from me. "I'm Wendy, by the way."

"I'm Gabriel, and this is Orson. Thanks for the coffee. I'm sorry, but until I met Sheila I thought that magic was... well..."

"Nonsense? Bullpucky? Hogswallop?" Wendy asked cheerfully.

Unlike Kathryn, she didn't seeming to be forcing herself to act nice. She showed genuine enthusiasm. I definitely was not used to that. "Um, yeah. No offense."

"None taken. Everyone likes to think they are completely rational until it suits them not to be. If you were to go out and ask the first ten people you met if they believed in magic, all ten would say no. But I bet at least half of them would have a rabbit-foot keychain or a four-leaf-clover charm on a bracelet. Or maybe they believe that if they sit in a certain chair with their hat at a certain angle, their team will win."

"That's superstition, not magic."

"It's all part of the same thing, dear. It's a remnant of the past, of old rituals. It's like why we decorate eggs at Easter. Show me where in the Bible Jesus talks about coloring eggs and hiding them. No, that's a leftover from the rituals of spring that the Christians co-opted. The ritual is to honor Ostara, the pagan goddess of spring, with a symbol of rebirth."

I took a sip of the coffee. The brew was much better than the gas-station and truck-stop stuff I had been drinking. "Thanks for the coffee. It's wonderful."

"I get the beans from a small batch roaster in Miami. He brought the roasting technique with him when he escaped from Cuba." She waved a hand. "But you're not here to talk about coffee."

"No. I need help."

"And how did you come to ask me?"

"I read about you in the Lakeland paper, about you getting fired from the college. The way you insisted that you were a witch and not a Wiccan reminded me of how Sheila phrased it."

"She sounds like a smart woman."

"She is, but she's in trouble. She's been missing for weeks."

Wendy cocked an eyebrow. "And how do I know that you aren't the reason she's missing?"

Ramona's smug smirk when she'd asked the same question had nearly made me fly off the handle. But even though Wendy had just met me, I didn't sense any malice in the question. I felt calm and comfortable around her. I reached down and patted Orson. "If you really are magic, you can just ask him."

Orson sat up and gave her his big, sad eyes. Wendy

scratched him on his head, and some drool dripped off his lower lip. Either he really liked her or he wanted more salami.

Wendy smiled. "You're right. If you had hurt her, her familiar wouldn't be hanging around you."

I nodded. "We've been trying to find her. She came down here to find something for her coven. They won't tell me what it was, but Orson and I are retracing her steps. We managed to follow her back to this guy named Yareth."

Wendy's smile vanished, and a scowl took its place. "I see. Yes, he was very intent on me joining his little gang. He promised that I would suffer the consequences if I didn't. He's a bit of a melodramatic twit."

"I've noticed."

"He does have some ability, but I had no intention of getting mixed up with his darkness. Besides, I didn't think he was strong enough to challenge me. I strengthened my shields and called it a day." She shook her head ruefully.

"But he did hurt you, didn't he?"

Her upper lip curled in a snarl. "Yes."

"Let me guess. He made an anonymous call to the college and found a right-wing Christian to talk to about the evil pagan in their midst."

She grinned. "Aren't you a smart one?"

"Not really. If I was, I wouldn't have let them give Orson a cookie full of drugs and kidnap him."

Wendy gasped and looked down at Orson. "Oh, you poor baby!" She picked him up and gave him a hug. "Wait. I know what you'll like." She set him down then went behind the counter and through a door that I assumed led to the kitchen.

"No one cares if I get hurt."

Orson drooled happily. *Poor baby.*

"What do you think of her?"

She has a good heart. Her aura reminds me of Sheila.

"Me too." If she knew Yareth, maybe she could help us

find out more about him, like where he might be hiding out.

Wendy came back with a bowl of broth and placed it on the floor in front of Orson. "Now, you eat that soup. It will get all the bad stuff out of you."

Orson tentatively lapped at the liquid then raised his head and grimaced.

"I know. It doesn't taste that good. But if you eat it all, you can have this." She brought her other hand out from behind her back. She held a stack of what looked like slices of roast beef and salami.

Orson whined but started lapping up the soup without further protest.

When Wendy sat back down, I asked, "So what's Yareth's deal?"

She sighed. "Other than being an asshole? He wants to be a big man. He wants to be the biggest magic user there is. He enjoys having people fawning all over him and stroking his ego. That's what it really comes down to."

"How long has he been in Florida?"

"The first time I met him was about a year ago. He popped up at our coven meeting."

"I didn't know men were welcome at covens."

"Who told you that?"

"That's been my experience."

Wendy shrugged. "Well, not necessarily. You never heard of a warlock? Sure, most covens are only women, but sympathetic men are welcome. Warlocks, too."

For the first time, it occurred to me that Sheila's coven members just didn't like me personally. "Sheila's coven doesn't exactly make me feel welcome. As a matter of fact, it's quite the opposite."

"Don't be too hard on them. A lot of women have good reason to distrust men, not to mention people in general. Goddess knows I wish we had been more distrustful of Yareth."

"People don't just pop up at covens, do they? The one at home is always going on about how secret they are." Of course, they might have had a good reason. If they were helping a jerk like Yareth, they might not be too eager to publicize that.

"Yes. You need to be invited to a meeting. Otherwise, you'll just kind of stumble past it. Like the trick your little dog does."

"But you saw through that when he tried it today."

"Yes, if you're more experienced, more powerful, you can see through most blocks."

Orson sat up, his eyes all sad. *Hey...*

Wendy reached down to stroke his neck, then she slipped him another piece of salami. "Oh, sorry. Your mama taught you well, and you're very strong, but I've been doing this a long time."

"So did someone invite Yareth to your meeting? Or is he just that powerful?"

Wendy looked thoughtful. "A bit of both, I'm afraid. One of our coven had a friend up north who told her that Yareth was coming our way. Her friend said that Yareth was very strong but troubled, and he could use some guidance. We were going to talk about letting him come to a meeting when he just showed up."

I remembered going to a coven meeting with Sheila for the first time. She made me wait in the front of the store while she talked to the others. I tried to follow her to the backroom, but each time I got close to the door, I was somehow distracted. There was always something across the room I had to see. Eventually, I forgot why I wanted to go back there so badly. Maybe that was why I never fully trusted the coven members. Sheila's word should have been enough for them to do away with all the secrecy.

"Who's the one who referred him to you? Can I talk to her?"

"The woman who brought him in is no longer in the coven. She left with him."

I slumped in the booth seat. "Oh." I straightened as an idea hit me. "Her name wouldn't be Madison, would it? Works at a vintage clothing store?"

Wendy stopped her coffee cup halfway to her lips. "My, you do get around."

"I ran into her last night. You're right. She's way into Yareth. Did any other members of the coven leave with her?"

"No, just her."

"Do you think I could talk to them? Do you think they might know any more about him?"

She shook her head. "After Yareth's little display at the meeting, they got spooked. You have to understand, most of them are just beginners. They are Wiccans who are trying on something a little more powerful. They have a very small amount of knowledge and magical talents. And after Yareth tried to ruin me professionally, they didn't think I would be able to protect them. So I shut things down and told the group to go to ground." She frowned. "It took me a while to find them all and to get them to trust me. I didn't like hiding, but it seemed the best thing to do until this all calmed down."

"Is it normal for a coven to have a bunch of beginners with only one or two people who are actually powerful?"

"Sure. You ever hear of the eighty-twenty rule?"

I shook my head. "No. What's that?"

"It's a rule of thumb in economics, which has real-world applications. Eighty percent of a business is generated by twenty percent of its customers. Eighty percent of the complaints come from twenty percent of the clients. Twenty percent of the employees make eighty percent of the sales."

I guessed the next part. "And twenty percent of the witches account for eighty percent of the magic."

"Yes! The coven member who told me that taught business classes at the college."

"I'm sorry about your job, by the way."

"Well, don't worry. I found a force more powerful than witchcraft or dark magic." She pointed toward the front window. "See that billboard across the street? Goldstein & Myers. They're my attorneys. They say it's a slam-dunk First Amendment case. They're quite confident the school will settle my wrongful termination suit out of court."

She stood up. "How about I freshen our coffees?"

"Yeah, that would be great." I started to slide out of the booth. "You need some help?"

"No. It's no problem." She smiled at Orson. "I'll bring you some water."

Orson chuffed and put on his doggie smile. I settled back into my seat.

Wendy returned a few minutes later with a bowl of water for Orson, which he began happily, and noisily, lapping. She placed a cup of coffee in front of me, and I did my best to act a little less enthusiastic than the dog, though it wasn't easy. That stuff was great.

She sat on the other side of the table and stirred her coffee. "Anyway, I put the coven on a bit of a hiatus. I have outside income, so things weren't so bad for me. I didn't want to risk him screwing around with their livelihoods."

I put my cup down. "So most covens would be similar to yours?"

"It's just a rule of thumb. I couldn't say for certain, but it would seem likely."

If Sheila's coven followed that rule, then only one or two other witches in that group were powerful. If I had to choose, I would bet Ramona was one of them.

I had stuck the rings in an old take-out bag from the car so I wouldn't lose any of them. I pulled the sack out of my pocket and passed it to Wendy. "There are five rings in here that Yareth seemed pretty concerned about. Can you tell me anything about them?"

Wendy took the bag and peeked inside. "What do you already know about them?"

"They were on display at the shop Yareth was using as a headquarters. I know one seems to act as a power boost. When Orson had it on his collar, it was the first time in weeks he could touch Sheila."

Wendy's brow furrowed. "You really shouldn't mess around with things you don't know anything about."

"You aren't the first one to tell me that."

Yeah. Orson perked up. *Maybe you could check them out for us.*

"Of course, sweetie, since you asked so nicely." Wendy scratched Orson's head, and his tongue lolled appreciatively. She shook the rings out of the bag and spread them out on the table. "Well, you probably don't have to worry. Magical artifacts, like magical people, are pretty rare."

She examined the rings, one at a time. Next, she closed her eyes and passed her hand over each one. She started with the green one. "Junk." The blue. "Junk." The yellow. "Tacky. And junk." She paused over the purple one, and her eyes popped open. "Now, this is something!"

I nodded. "That's the one Orson had on."

"Yes, it seems to be quite strong." She closed her eyes again. "I can feel the energy radiating off of it." She frowned and opened her eyes again. She pointed at the base of the stone where it met the metal of the ring. "See these scratches and gouges? It was hacked out of something bigger. And not very cleanly." She clucked disapprovingly. "Sometimes bigger is better. If this came from a much larger stone, then that original stone could be incredibly powerful."

"How much more powerful?" I asked.

"It depends on how big it is. If the original is as big as a golf ball, it could be three times as strong."

If that rock was three times stronger than that ring, it might be enough for Orson to touch Sheila again and help him to stay in contact with her. Orson shivered. I understood completely. He had been almost overwhelmed by the ring.

Wendy moved on to the orange one. When her hand hovered over it, she frowned. "Well, there is something here. But it's not magical."

She stood and walked over to the counter. She bent down then straightened, holding a baseball bat in her hand. When I raised an eyebrow, she explained. "Drunk frat boys don't always respond to spells." She returned to our table. "You might want to get up and stand back."

I scooted out and stood about a foot away. Orson took the hint and came over to sit behind me. Wendy separated the orange ring from the others, raised the bat over her head, and brought it down on the offending jewelry. The cheap tin broke, and the stone shattered, revealing a familiarly shaped piece of metal and plastic.

I scooped it up and stared at it. It was some kind of tracker device. And I had cheerfully planted it on myself.

Orson chuffed. *Told you so.*

Even though the restaurant was chilled from the air conditioning, I felt sweat running down my back. I tried to retrace my steps in my mind to figure out if someone had followed us. I didn't remember seeing anyone at the rest stop that morning. But if Yareth could hide Orson from me in a storeroom I was standing in, he could probably hide a car that was tailing us. I spun around, trying to see all the windows at once.

Wendy grabbed my arm. "Take it easy. I don't sense anything bad out there. No one's followed you. At least not yet."

I drew in a long breath. Perhaps Yareth had put Madison

110

in charge of tracking us. That would be okay because she had other problems to contend with at the moment.

At my request, Wendy smashed the green, blue, and yellow rings in a similar fashion. They were just what they appeared to be: cheap costume jewelry. I wanted to crack open the purple stone as well, but Wendy didn't.

She held up the ring. "Yareth surely knows that if he tampered with the ring, he might affect the stone's magical properties."

"I only had the purple ring last night."

"He may have just followed you. If he had put something in that ring, the magic wouldn't have worked so well for Orson."

Still, I insisted on inspecting the base of the ring. It seemed to be in one piece. I couldn't spot any splits or glue bubbles. That still left the problem of what to do with the tracker.

"I'm so sorry," I told her. "I didn't want to drag you into this. I was just trying to get some answers."

"Well, I was already involved. And I can certainly handle Yareth."

Someone knocked on the door. Orson and I both jumped.

Wendy laughed. "Oh, that's just the lunch rush." She hopped up and walked over to the front of the store.

I scooped up all of the ring debris and dumped it back into the sack. I put the purple ring in one pocket and the tracker in the other.

Wendy unlocked the front door and flipped the sign back to Open. A couple of guys in baseball caps and flip-flops came in.

"Hi, Wendy. Everything okay?" one asked.

"Oh, fine. Just having a little business meeting. What can I get for you, Frank? Tuna on a spelt roll, like usual?"

He gave her a wink. "You know it."

Wendy headed back behind the counter. "Sorry, boys,"

she called to Orson and me, "but a gal's gotta make a living."

I didn't want to leave just yet, so I got in line and ordered an Abra-Capicola sandwich. Morty's dognapping money was certainly coming in handy.

As she handed me the sandwich and my change, she leaned over the counter and whispered, "I'll do all I can to help you find her. Come back tonight, and I may have an idea." She passed me a business card with her number on it. "Give me a call if anything comes up."

I nodded and thanked her. Orson and I left the restaurant as the rest of the lunch rush began to file in.

TWENTY-ONE

W E WALKED DOWN THE BLOCK to a minor league stadium I had seen on the way. I thought about Tom, one of my squad members, and how he used to talk about wanting to be a professional baseball player. He would never get there. I frequently checked over my shoulder for any black-clad minions that might be tailing us. I didn't spot anyone suspicious.

There were a couple of buses in the lot. One was a team bus for the St. Lucie Mets. I fished the chip out of my pocket and stuck it to the bumper with some discarded gum. Port St. Lucie was on the other side of the state and a three-hour drive away. Yareth and company could have a fun road trip to watch the horrible future big leaguers.

I was glad Wendy promised to help us because I was fresh out of ideas. But her shop didn't close until seven. I didn't want to hang out in that area, so I decided to drive around for a while and think about where to go to kill some time. We headed back to the car.

A garbage truck was rolling up the street. In a fit of paranoia, I pitched the fart phone in a nearby can. I was tired of the constant text messages, anyway.

When we got to the front of the store, Orson sniffed around the car to make sure no one had tampered with it. *All clear.* He hopped in when I opened the passenger door, only having to scramble a little with one back paw to get into the seat.

I grunted as I climbed behind the wheel. My back was stiff from napping at the rest stop. I leaned from side to side to stretch, then I rolled my head to loosen up my neck. As I did, I glimpsed something in the side mirror: a red Honda parked about a block behind us.

It couldn't have been Madison. She had to be in the hospital. I was just jumpy. Hondas were pretty popular, and there were lots of red cars.

I put the car in gear and entered the line of traffic. The red Honda pulled out onto the road as well. I told myself that it had to be a coincidence. After all, we were on the main road back to I-4. There were plenty of reasons for a common model of a popular car to be driving toward a busy highway.

But I didn't like coincidences. The light ahead was yellow, so I pulled around a slow-moving pickup, into the lane for oncoming traffic, and gunned it. Narrowly avoiding a head-on collision with an SUV, I swerved back into the right lane and turned hard onto the westbound on-ramp. I checked the rearview mirror. The Honda hadn't made the light.

Maybe I was just being paranoid. I rubbed my eyes. Wendy's coffee was wearing off. I glanced over at Orson. He was drooling on the seat and panting from the noontime sun beaming through the passenger window. The poor dog had been through a lot, and he was still not back to full strength. I decided a nap would do us both some good.

I checked my side view mirror to get into the right lane for the next exit so I could find a cheap motel. A red Honda was two cars behind me. It couldn't possibly be the same car.

A high-speed car chase was not something I wanted at the moment. If I was being followed, I needed to lose them quickly. An eighteen-wheeler was lumbering onto the highway just ahead, and that gave me an idea. The on-ramp was just in front of the exit, making for a tricky merge. I stomped on the gas pedal to speed up and get next to the semi. At the last possible second, I cut in front of him to take the exit. Orson bumped into the door and barked his displeasure. The truck driver laid on the horn and slammed on his brakes, but the dangerous maneuver worked. The body of the truck blocked the view of the exit from the other cars long enough for me to get off the highway.

I watched the exit ramp in the side mirror. No red Honda came down it.

Just because we're in Florida doesn't mean you have to drive like it!

"Sorry, pal."

I stretched in the seat, and a billboard caught my eye. I decided it might be safer to go to a more public place to regroup. "You hungry?"

I could eat.

"Great. You can dig yourself up a snack when we get to Dinosaur World."

The Dinosaur World sign promised over one hundred fifty life-sized dinosaur statues in twenty acres of park in nearby Plant City, twenty miles west of our location. That sounded like a good place to get away for a while. There would be lots of space to think, and Orson could try to intimidate the Tyrannosaurus rex. He wouldn't even need to hide himself. Friendly dogs were welcome.

I didn't see any more Hondas. Orson barked at me more than once to tell me to get my eyes off the rearview mirror and onto the road.

Can't help Mama if you get squashed.

I spotted a rare payphone outside a gas station and pulled into the parking lot. Crossing my fingers that the thing actually worked, I got out of the car and walked over to the phone. I missed the fart phone already. Surprisingly, the payphone seemed to be in fairly good condition. Keeping an eye out for any more red Hondas, I pulled out the card and called Wendy.

She answered after a few rings, sounding a little out of breath. "This is the Sand Witch. How can I help you?"

"Wendy, it's Gabriel."

"Oh, Gabriel, I'm sorry. I'm still working."

"I know. I just wanted to fill you in on what's happening." I told her all about seeing the red Honda outside her store and who I thought the car might belong to. "I don't know how it could be Madison, after all the stuff she took. But you should be careful, just in case."

"It was probably nothing," Wendy said. "Probably. I still haven't felt any bad presences. I'll keep an eye out, though."

I yawned. "I have to get some rest, but I don't want to be napping in a rest stop again in case Madison comes back. We're going to hang out with some big, intimidating dinosaurs."

"Yeah, I think you guys staying in a public place is a good idea. I'll see you at seven."

When we arrived at Dinosaur World, the parking lot wasn't nearly as full as I had hoped. I wanted to blend in with a crowd. But maybe with twenty acres to get lost in, it wouldn't matter. I put the sandwich I bought from Wendy in my pocket then got the leash out of the glove compartment.

Orson gave me a sad look. *That's ridiculous.*

"You know they have leash laws. I'll take it off once we get through the gate."

He reluctantly let me snap it to his collar. *You owe me for this.*

"Hey, you're getting to go see giant dinosaur bones. What more could a dog want?"

He chuffed and tugged me toward the gate. *Let's get this over with.*

We didn't have any problems getting through the gate.

We walked a good ways into the park before I chose a bench with a view of a triceratops the size of an SUV. I took off the leash, and Orson tried to stare the dinosaur down until I pulled the sandwich out of my pocket. I split off a third of it and pinched it into bite-size morsels before piling it in front of him.

You promised me fossils.

"You would chip your teeth. Stick with the capicola."

I started munching on the remainder of the sandwich, which turned out to be even better than the coffee. The area we were in was pretty much deserted, so I felt safe enough to relax a bit.

Yareth was fairly new in town, but he seemed to have been making quite a name for himself as a magical douchebag. He was also apparently one of the few who had some actual magical talent. But he wasn't using it in a positive way. A cocky attitude and actual ability was a combination that made it very easy for a person to bite off more than he could handle and wind up hurting himself or others.

Even worse was the possibility that he knew exactly what he was doing. If he wasn't just showing off for a circle of admirers, he could truly be trying to become the most powerful person he could be, and he wouldn't blink before hurting anyone who got in his way. Capturing and controlling Sheila demonstrated that he was pretty powerful already.

Sheila had told me a little about black magic. "Witches work in the light. We practice white magic. We don't try to hurt others. We use defensive spells. We don't send out curses. Magic isn't to be used like a parlor trick. We aren't supposed to use it to make ourselves rich, like by fixing the lottery or something."

"Why not?" I had asked.

"Aside from the fact that theft is wrong and hurting others is bad?"

I felt my face go red. "Uh, sure, besides that."

"It takes a toll on you. It's like your soul is a ledger. Every time you use magic for evil, it makes a mark on you. Before long, your soul is full of black marks, and that corrupts you. Darkness colors your worldview and your actions, and before long, you only think about how others can be used to help yourself. I've seen people who've gone that way. It's not pretty."

"Went to the dark side, they did?"

Sheila closed her eyes and rubbed the bridge of her nose. "It's annoying that you have to filter everything through *Star Wars*, but yes. It's essentially like going to the dark side of the Force."

"I'll be very upset if you tell me you're my sister."

"Ha. Stop it. This is serious. Magic is difficult, and doing the right thing is hard as well. Every day, people just do the easy thing and act selfishly. They drop a gum wrapper on the street rather than go five feet out of their way to put it in a trash can. They hit the Close Door button on an elevator when someone is running up because they don't want to wait an extra ten seconds. Imagine how tempting it could be to use magic to eliminate any obstacle in your way. If someone drives too slow in front of you and you could just push them out of the way? Or if a rival for a promotion could conveniently disappear? Do you know how easy it can be to just let go of all your morality and judgment and just... just...?"

I took her hand. Yes, I knew. I had gotten a medal for knowing. "I'm sorry."

"I'm sorry, too. I know you know." She wiped away a tear. "That's why Orson is so great. Familiars remind you that you aren't alone. And sometimes, they can make the hard choices for you."

"What do you mean?"

She took a breath. "One night, my stepfather was

drunk. He had been eyeing me all night. I hated that look. I knew what would come next."

I had to remind myself to breathe.

"After I went to bed, I heard him lurching up the stairs. I started to cry. Mr. Whiskers slipped out the door. A few seconds later, there was a loud crash. Mr. Whiskers came back in the room, jumped on the bed, and started grooming himself. I got up and went to see what had happened. My stepfather was lying at the bottom of the stairs."

"He fell?"

"Mr. Whiskers never said otherwise, but I had a feeling my stepfather's fall was no accident. Mr. Whiskers was protecting me any way he could. My stepdad never walked right again. Even better, he couldn't climb stairs, so he had to sleep in the living room. I left home pretty soon after that."

I was amazed. And after I thought about it, I was also a little concerned about all the times that cat had tried to trip me.

"But Mr. Whiskers was never quite the same, either. Even though he had been protecting me, and protecting me from something evil, hurting a person still marked him. He always loved it when I petted him, but after that fall, he sometimes shuddered when I touched him, almost like he felt dirty about it."

Like that cat, Orson would sacrifice himself to help Sheila. I knew that. I would do the same. I just hoped it didn't come down to that for either of us.

We took turns napping on the bench. One always stayed awake to keep watch.

TWENTY-TWO

ON THE WAY OUT, I stopped to look around in the gift shop. They sold replica velociraptor claws. I bought one with Morty's money. The claw had a pleasing weight, and the thought of hitting Yareth upside the head with it gave me no small amount of pleasure. The image of slicing him somewhere delicate was even better.

The early evening traffic was light, and we made good time back to Lakeland. At a little after seven, I turned onto the street where the Sand Witch was located. At least five people were standing in a semicircle in front of the store. I rolled to a stop and peered down the road. I thought about putting the top up, but I was afraid to draw any attention. Also, with the top down, we could hear better. I scrunched down behind the wheel a bit, just enough so that I could still peek over the dash.

I recognized three of the people: Yareth, pointy beard and all; Madison, apparently having recovered from her overdose; and little Morty. I guessed the gators hadn't been very hungry, or perhaps they just weren't interested in eating something so greasy. Morty's hands and one arm were covered in bandages.

Yareth called out, "Come now, Wendy. We know he was here. Where did he go? Why don't you just make it easy on yourself?"

From behind the screen door, Wendy responded, "Blow it out your ass, Criss Angel!"

Orson growled in support. He was ready to leap into the fray.

Yareth chuckled. "Oh, Wendy. It is *adorable* that you think your shields can withstand me. In a few minutes, we'll be inside. And we'll find out all your secrets."

I rolled my eyes. I couldn't wait to interrogate that guy with a few good punches.

Yareth took a step forward and held out his hands. A large purple stone about the size and shape of a toy football glowed in his palms. If that was the same rock the ring had been made from, Wendy's estimate of a golf-ball-sized one being three times stronger was out the window. That thing was probably fifteen or twenty times more powerful than the ring. And if it had the same effect, I doubted Wendy could hold out for long. The two acolytes I hadn't met moved to stand beside Yareth. They each put a hand on their leader's shoulders. Morty and Madison laid their hands on the shoulders of the other two, making a five-person chain. They all began to chant in unison.

I couldn't make out what they were saying. "Orson, what the hell's going on?"

He closed his eyes. *Wendy has shields to keep out magical intruders. Yareth is combining the energies of his followers to get through.*

"Can he do it?"

Wendy is strong, so normally, I would say no, but...

"What?"

There's something else, the same energy I felt when I had that ring yesterday. I don't know what it is.

A loud crack came from the store sign. The head of the witch logo crumpled as if being crushed in a fist.

Wow. I've never seen anything like that.

"Me, neither," I whispered.

From the shock on Wendy's face, she hadn't, either. She raised her hands as if to hold the roof up by herself.

"We've got to help her." I grabbed the blackjack out of

the glove compartment and raced out of the car, with Orson following through the open door. We sprinted toward the group of witches. If the five of them together were what made them so powerful, then maybe we could even things out a little. Fortunately, the little group was too intent on crushing the sandwich shop to notice us approaching.

"Orson, the girl on the end!" I pointed at Madison. "She's the one who kidnapped you last night. Tell her thank you."

Growling, Orson took off. If a chain was as strong as its weakest link, I had a pretty good idea that gator bait was it. I barreled toward Morty.

Orson sank his teeth into Madison's leg. She screamed and let go of her coven-mate as she tried to hop away from Orson. A second later, I cracked Morty over the head with my blackjack. When he started to turn, I kicked his bad leg, and he went down like a sack of potatoes.

The next two in line faced us. I didn't recognize the one nearest me, but I also didn't stop to introduce myself. I swung the sap hard across his jaw. The loud crack was pretty satisfying.

Madison was still screaming and trying to shake Orson off her leg. The fourth witch was trying to pull him off her. *Good luck with that.* I could waste the better part of an hour trying to get a chew toy out of his mouth.

Yareth didn't seem to be bothered by the fact that he was standing alone. The noise and light seemed to drain from my surroundings as he focused on me with a sick grin on his face. "At last we meet face to face. Thank you for bringing the dog back to me. You saved me the trouble of tracking him down."

I started to swing the blackjack, but the weapon felt so heavy in my hand. So heavy... I couldn't hold on to it. I lowered my arm. I scarcely felt the blackjack leave my hand, and the soft thud as it hit the grass was barely audible.

Yareth nodded. "That's right. You shouldn't carry such heavy things. They can tire you out."

Yes, tired. I'd been going all day. I was so tired. I couldn't stand up any longer. I slumped down to my knees.

"Poor boy. You just sit right there. I'll handle the rest."

Sitting was such a good idea. It had been years since I sat down. My body felt as if a thousand pounds of concrete were pressing down on me. I rocked back onto my heels.

Ow! I shook my head. *What was that?* Something was poking me in the ass. I reached back and pulled the offending item from my back pocket. The raptor claw! Before Yareth could mess with my head again, I flung the claw at him. If he hadn't moved his head at the last second, the sharp end would have gouged out his eye, but it still left a nice bloody gash down his cheek. I leapt at him and tried to swat the stone out of his hands, but he had a kung-fu grip on it. He took a swing at my head and missed. I punched him in the face and got in a good hit on the same spot where he'd been cut with the talon.

Yareth yelped and rocked backward. He clapped a hand to his cheek, but blood poured through his fingers. He appeared to be in shock, as if it was beyond his comprehension that he might be the one bleeding. He clearly hadn't expected any resistance.

I started after him, but I had taken only two steps when someone cracked me on the back of my head. I lurched forward, stumbled, and fell to my knees. I had been so wrapped up with fighting Yareth that I'd forgotten about the others. The minion who'd been trying to pull Orson off of Madison had come to help her boss.

"Orson! Come here!" I yelled.

Orson let go of Madison. She tried to kick his backside as he headed for me, but her foot missed him by several inches. Snarling, Orson ran over and snapped at my attacker. The girl backed off and ran with Yareth to one of the cars. I tried to get up and follow, but my vision was a little blurry.

Madison lurched to her feet. She must have put too much weight back on her bitten leg because she whimpered a little. She hobbled over to the one whose jaw I'd broken and helped him over to the second car. The coven convoy drove off with a screech of tires.

That left poor, unconscious Morty with us. Orson kept watch on him.

Feeling pretty woozy, I got to my feet and went to the restaurant door to check on Wendy. "Are you all right?" I asked her.

Her face was pale. "I think so." She came outside to survey the damage to her place. "Thank Goddess you showed up. They came just as the store closed. I was sure that I could keep them at bay, but I... I've never seen that much power."

That was getting to be a common refrain. "They were tearing your roof off. That's not normal for witches, I take it?"

Wendy laughed. The sound was bitter and angry, nothing like her joyful laugh of that morning. "No. That's not supposed to happen. I've heard stories, legends about witches of old who had that kind of power. But those are just fairy tales. I mean, really fairy stories."

Orson went over to sniff at Morty and growled when the man whimpered. *He's still alive. Should I send for more gators?*

"No. They're too unreliable." I turned back to Wendy. "Hey, if you don't mind helping us, I think I have something bigger in mind."

TWENTY-THREE

DINOSAUR WORLD DIDN'T HAVE THE best security. After all, no one was going to try to steal a twenty-foot dinosaur. Wendy and Orson put the two security guards to sleep without any problems. Carrying the unconscious Morty wasn't fun, but goth kids were pretty scrawny, so I managed.

We found a suitable tree near the bench Orson and I had sat on earlier. I used the last of the rope from the car to tie Morty to the tree. *Reminder: stop at Home Depot tomorrow.* I slipped off Orson's collar, looped it in the magic booster ring, and put it back on him. He got that glazed look for a second, but he soon bobbed his head to indicate he was good to go. I slapped Morty hard across the face. Sure, Wendy probably could have reversed the spell she'd put him under to keep him unconscious, but slapping him was way more fun.

He came around slowly until he recognized me and Orson, then his eyes bulged. He started to struggle against the ropes, but I had tied them pretty tightly. "Get away from me!"

"Is that any way to talk? Your buddies just ditched you and left you to die in the street."

"You tried to feed me to alligators!"

"Potato, po-tah-to."

"What?"

I shook my head. "I'm curious. Just how did you get

back here?" As a Boy Scout, I had earned a knot badge, so I knew he hadn't gotten free on his own.

That seemed to awaken the young asshat that I knew and loved. "Oh, you fool. There are so many things you don't understand."

I bent over to get my face level with his. "You know, Morty, you guys should really learn when to shut the fuck up with the mystical bullshit and just give a straight answer. You and your pals have been a major pain in my ass, and I'm tired of it."

"So what? What else are you going to do to me?"

I smirked. "You think you're the only one who's special?" I straightened and nodded at Orson and Wendy.

Wendy put her hand on Orson's neck to make contact with the ring. They focused on Morty, and their eyes began to glow. I turned back to our captive. Morty looked around wildly, then he screamed.

I knew if I looked back, I wouldn't see anything out of the ordinary. But I was certain Morty was getting an eyeful. I walked over and touched Orson so I could see the illusion, too.

The twenty-foot T. rex was walking toward Morty. I could feel the pounding of its footsteps. The giant lizard leaned over Morty. I smelled urine and looked down to see a wet stain spreading across the guy's crotch.

I stepped back over to the tree. "Now, you're going to answer a few questions. My friends can control this guy a lot better than the gators. Plus, that T. rex has gotta be pretty hungry. He hasn't eaten in sixty-five million years."

Morty flinched and tried to move his head. "Ah! Okay! Just get it away from me!"

I could no longer see the dinosaur, but I guessed it had just tried to bite off Morty's head. I gestured at Wendy. She gave me a wicked little grin. Morty slumped in his bindings, and I guessed the T. rex had backed off a bit.

I crouched in front of Morty. "Tell me about Yareth and your playgroup."

"I met him a month ago. Madison worked at Mom's store, and he came in to meet her."

A month ago was when Sheila had travelled to Florida for the first time. "So how did you get involved?"

"He wanted a place to have meetings. Madison suggested our storeroom. I told them that I could convince Mom. Madison said she'd be so grateful if I could do it."

Ah. If there was anything more likely to lead a young man astray than black magic, it was that ol' black magic: love. Or lust, at least. "How many of you are there?"

"About a dozen. But Yareth's been recruiting. Maddie said it was just the two of them for a while, but things have really picked up recently."

"Is that because of the stone?"

Morty hesitated. I moved over to touch Orson's collar again because I wanted to see the giant dinosaur snap at little Morty's head. The T. rex did not disappoint. Flecks of dino-spittle flew everywhere. I even felt the air rush past my face when the creature roared.

"Okay! Make it stop!" Morty sounded as if he might pee his pants again.

The dinosaur stepped back. I let go of Orson's collar. "All right. Talk."

"He had the stone when I met him. He said it was sent to him from the depths of Hell, and it was a sign that he would command the forces of magic on this plane."

That sounded like a bad parody of Lovecraft, but Morty seemed to really believe it. And that stone did have power. I had seen it in action. But I didn't think Hell had anything to do with it. "Good. Now, tell me about Sheila."

Morty furrowed his brow. "Who?" Then he screamed and cringed. The T. rex must have been getting awfully close.

"The girl you saw at the store. The one Yareth was fighting with."

"Aaaah!" Morty squirmed, eyes bulging. "I don't know where she is. Keep it back!"

I waved a hand. Morty closed his eyes and started screaming. They must have had the dino practically licking him on the cheek. I gestured again, and a couple of minutes later, Morty opened one eye.

I knelt and got in his face. "Where is Sheila?"

"I don't know! I swear! Yareth just said she was bait. He said she's a candle that will draw you all in like moths to a flame."

Well, that was something. Sheila had to be alive. And Yareth had her. "Thank you, Morty. And what's all this about feeding you to the gators? I left you a knife, didn't I?"

"You try working a knife when your hands are tied. Those things took a piece out of my arm. I almost lost a finger!"

I had noticed the bandage on his hand, but it seemed like he was overselling it. "Too bad. Learn to jack off with the other hand."

"Yareth knows when I'm in trouble. He knows when any of his followers are hurt. He knows where we are at all times."

He sees you when you're sleeping. Creepier than Santa Claus. Hopefully, Yareth was too busy licking his wounds to worry about Morty for the moment. "So he sent someone to get you?"

"He came himself. He cares about us. And he won't stop until he gets what he wants."

"Well, you better hope they come for you again."

"What? Why would—"

Wendy reached into Morty's head and put him to sleep again. "The guards will find him in the morning."

She and Orson looked over at the dinosaur. The T. rex

128

came to life in front of my eyes and waved at me with its tiny arm.

I blinked and took a step back. Orson and Wendy shared a laugh. I hustled them out of there before they decided it would be funny to make some raptors come after me.

TWENTY-FOUR

I WASN'T THRILLED ABOUT LEAVING A minion for Yareth, but I remembered what Sheila had told me: killing left a mark. I had scarred up my soul badly enough that I didn't need any unnecessary blood on my hands. Dinosaur nightmares would have to be punishment enough.

We pulled into the parking lot of a burger place with outdoor tables. Wendy took Orson to the deserted patio while I went in and ordered us some food. I brought the laden tray out and sat down with them. Orson whined at the plain burger, but that dog's digestive system really didn't need any cheese.

After swallowing a bit of my burger, I asked Wendy, "Was Yareth always that powerful?"

"No. Last year, when he crashed our meeting, he had some ability and strength, but it was pretty raw, mostly just bluster. He was certainly way more hat than cattle, as my dad would say. But now that he has that stone..."

"I don't know a lot about magic stones, but based on that display, I'd guess that you were right. Bigger is better."

Orson snorted. *Good guess.*

"Morty said Yareth's had that stone at least as long as he's known him. So he got it sometime in the last few months."

Wendy nodded. She had become much quieter since

that morning. "So, the question would be where he got it." She glanced at her watch.

Orson finished his burger and whined. *Mama first came down here a month ago. Yareth has been recruiting heavily for a month.*

I gaped at him. "Do you think that stone was what she was trying to find?"

I haven't seen anything else here worth coming here for. Aside from the capicola.

Wendy stroked his head. "Thanks, boy."

The timeline definitely matched up. Sheila's trip, her run-in with Yareth, the beginning of Team Yareth. The stone and the ring. Maybe Sheila knew how to control that stone.

"Have you ever seen a stone like that before?" I asked Wendy. "Or even read about one?"

"Well, I used to teach a section on Native American religions. There were stories about Stonecoats, stone giants. One legend had a stonecoat rub something on a young brave's hands and feet, and it made him strong. The stories said it was a bone, but it could have been a rock or a crystal."

"Do you think it could be that?"

She shrugged. "Most legends are just that. Legends. And that was a Seneca legend. They were in New York state, not Florida. I don't know of any Seminole tales like that. But the stone could easily be a native artifact. It could be something brought over from Europe or Mexico by the Conquistadors. It could have been something they took from a witch in the Inquisition. It could have been found when they dug up the foundation for a shopping mall in Daytona." She shook her head. "But it's not something I'm familiar with."

Doesn't matter. It's what Mama was after. And Yareth got it first.

I reached down and patted Orson's head. "We'll find

her. We're closer than ever. We know she's here. Yareth knows where she is."

We thought that last night. And last week.

"I know."

TWENTY-FIVE

Wendy insisted on going back to Lakeland. I tried to get her to go somewhere else, but she would have none of it. "That shop has been my family's home for sixty years. No two-bit magician is getting me to leave, magic stone or no magic stone."

"But he might come back."

"Let him! I haven't used all of my tricks yet. If he thinks that will work twice on me, he's in for a shock." She cracked her knuckles and started murmuring under her breath.

When she stopped, I asked her about something that had been bothering me. "I put that little bug on a bus heading over toward the east coast. Why did he show up at your place?"

She shook her head. "He said he knew you had been there recently. Maybe the tracker thingie just has a short range, so my shop was the last place that registered as a stop you made."

She was most likely right. But then again, maybe the Honda I had seen earlier that morning really had been Madison's. Yeah, I was getting paranoid, but I probably should have been a little more paranoid since the beginning. As they said, it's not paranoia if they're really out to get you. "Morty said that Yareth could find his followers wherever they were."

She shrugged. "That's not uncommon. I'll bet Orson

and Sheila could touch each other from miles away as well."

Orson chuffed in agreement. *Yes, almost anywhere.*

"Well, he kind of got in my head during that fight back at your place. He gave me this weird feeling, like I was completely exhausted and had to sit down. If that souvenir raptor talon hadn't poked me"—I saw no reason to go into detail about *where* I'd gotten jabbed—"things might have gone a lot differently. So I'm getting pretty worried. Since he got in my head once, can he get in again?"

Wendy looked thoughtful for a moment. "If you had asked me that yesterday, I would have said no. That kind of contact is usually possible only if you're incredibly strong. But the stone is making him much more powerful. I don't know for sure." She leaned down and rubbed Orson's head. "But don't worry. Orson is strong. He can keep you safe."

Yeah, I'll tuck you in and everything.

"I'm serious, pal. I don't need that guy playing around in my head and making me do things. What if he tries to make me hurt you?"

"Gabriel, he just made you feel tired, which you already were. So he amped up a feeling you already had. I'm guessing he wouldn't be able to make you do something completely outside your character."

"Well, I hope you're right."

As I parked in front of the store, Wendy sighed. "Thank you for your help. If you two hadn't shown up when you did, my store would be in a lot worse shape than it is. I'll do everything I can to help you find Sheila." She gave Orson another quick pat. "Familiars really do have a strong bond. If Orson could touch Sheila once, he can do it again. Maybe he needs a boost."

Orson drooled happily.

She smiled down at him. "If we combine our energy, maybe we can touch her and get a better fix on her." She surveyed her beat-up store again. "But first I have to see just how bad the damage is here." She opened her car door. "Gabriel, you're welcome to stay on my couch tonight, and I'm sure I could scrounge up a comfy pillow for Orson."

Ignoring Orson's whine, I said, "No. Your shop has already gotten one beating, thanks to me. We'll find another motel, somewhere farther away."

She climbed out of the car and leaned in to kiss Orson's nose. "I promised to help you find Sheila, and I will. I owe that little creep." She closed the door and headed for her store.

After Wendy had waved from inside the shop, I looked through the maps and coupon books I'd picked up to find a hotel.

While I sifted through them, Orson made his demands known. *Make sure they have breakfast waffles and HBO.*

Just because we were on the run didn't mean we had to rough it. We found a Super 8 in Winter Haven that fit the bill. I'd spent most of the last two days in the car. I really needed a hot shower and some sleep. I also needed a change of underwear, but all my clothes were back at the Hotel Ambush.

We stopped at Walmart to get some clothes for me and some Milk-Bones for Orson. I was tired of tracking down payphones. Fortunately, the store had a good selection of disposable ones. I bought a couple of them so I would have a spare.

Shopping finished, I drove to the hotel and checked us in at our new temporary digs. Inside the room, Orson cautiously sniffed everything while I opened the package with the phone.

"Hello, Lisa."

"Gabriel! Do you have any news? Did you find Sheila in Mississippi?"

"I never got there. I ran into Yareth before I could go."

"Oh." She sounded disappointed. I hoped it was

because we hadn't found Sheila and not because I was still alive. Or because she was going to be in trouble for feeding someone bad information about my whereabouts.

"Funny thing, though. He had this big purple rock that seemed to make him incredibly powerful."

"He had *what*?"

"A purple stone. And strangely, he seems to have picked it up at around the same time that Sheila came down here." When Lisa didn't respond, I said, "That's not a coincidence, is it? Sheila came down to get that stone, didn't she?"

"I can't say."

I was ready to throw the phone at a wall. "Of course you can. You just did. If she didn't come for that rock, you would have just said no."

Lisa was silent.

"What does this stone do? Yareth almost ripped the roof of a house off with it, and everyone keeps telling me it's impossible for him to do that."

"It is impossible! That kind of thing..."

"This guy is bad news. If he is anywhere close to Sheila, she's in real danger."

"That's not true. She can handle herself."

"Can you ask around about this guy? I found out that he only came down to Florida about a year ago. Before that, he was *up north*, which could mean anywhere between Virginia and Canada."

"I'll try, but you know how the coven can be. I shouldn't even be talking to you. How do you know where he's from?"

"I found some locals down here who met him. They said one of their coven members knew him."

"Why don't you just ask the coven member?"

"Well, we're not on the best of terms. Her name is Madison. Last night, she kidnapped Orson and almost killed herself rather than tell me where her great leader was. Today, she was part of Yareth's bunch when he almost destroyed a building. And I can't wait to see what happens tomorrow."

Lisa gasped. "Did you say *Madison*? Is she in her twenties? Shoulder-length brown hair?"

"Yeah, that's her."

Lisa sighed. "I think I know her. She's my cousin."

I opened and closed my mouth for a second before anything came out. "Your cousin? You didn't think it might be important to tell me you had a witch cousin in Florida?"

"Witches respect each other's privacy. I would never have thought to tell you about her unless she wanted me to. And frankly, I haven't spoken to her in almost a year. What did you mean when you said she tried to kill herself? How?"

"Well, maybe she wasn't actually trying to kill herself, but what she did was pretty dangerous. She swallowed a fistful of pills rather than tell me where Orson was. She seems fine now, though. She was healthy enough to help cast that spell with Yareth earlier."

"What is Madison doing with him?" She sounded more worried than angry, as though it might not be the first time Madison had done something dumb.

"Nothing good that I've seen. Was she into dognapping and black magic the last time you saw her?"

"No. She was never... I mean... no." She swallowed audibly. "She visited me in New York right when Sheila was getting me away from David. My aunt was having problems of her own, and Maddie was having a rough time with her. We helped prop each other up."

"So she seemed fine then?"

"Yes. Completely. She and Sheila helped me move into my new place."

I remembered when Sheila helped Lisa move out. Sheila always came home exhausted because Lisa had been a wreck and needed a lot of support. "So Madison knew Sheila? And Orson?"

"I don't think she ever actually met Orson, but one time you came to pick up Sheila from my place and you brought Orson. Maddie watched you guys from the window and commented on how well Sheila and Orson got along, how much in sync they were. I told her about familiars and explained how they help witches focus their power. She was very interested in that."

I was glad I'd bought two burner phones because I was going to crush the one in my hand into powder. "What happened to respecting a witch's privacy?"

"I'm sorry. She's my cousin. She was just starting out on the path and was very confused. My aunt is a piece of work, usually drunk and always nasty. If witchcraft was calming Madison down and helping her take control of her life, then I was happy to answer her questions about it."

Right. But I have to beg for a straight answer. I bit my tongue.

"And if I had known that she was going to use that knowledge for dark ends, I never would have told her. I'm so sorry."

"Well, at least now I know how they knew about Orson and why they want him so badly. Lisa told some dopey kid how special he is."

"Gabe, I know you wouldn't hurt Sheila. I do. She trusts you."

Sheila also told me Lisa made a lot of bad choices, but I didn't think I needed to bring that up. "Can you do something for me?"

"Yes. What do you need?"

That was good. She wasn't hedging her support anymore. "First, tell me where Madison's mom lives. Maybe she knows something more about this, like about the guy her daughter's spending all her time with."

"Sure. Her name is Judith Wilkins. She lives in a trailer

park just outside of Sarasota. It's called Happy Acres."
She gave me an address.

I checked my map. Sarasota was on the coast, about
two hours away. "Thanks. Second, please ask around
about Yareth. He came from somewhere up there, and
maybe somebody knows something about him. I know
the coven doesn't want to help, but maybe you can tell
them about the connection with Madison and how you're
worried about your poor cousin and Sheila."

Lisa sighed. "I really don't think it will go anywhere,
but I'll ask."

"Thank you, Lisa. Someone else thanks you, too." I
help the phone in front of Orson's mouth. He slobbered
out a *mama* for her. I put the phone back to my ear. "Did
you hear that?"

Lisa sniffed. "Emotional blackmail is dirty pool."

I told her I would call back the next day, and we hung
up. I turned on the TV for Orson. Orson happily watched
Game of Thrones while I collapsed on the bed. He liked the
dragons. I fell asleep almost immediately.

TWENTY-SIX

THE NEXT MORNING, I AWOKE to an odd noise. I jumped up and stared all around the room, ready to attack whoever was there.

Orson had been chewing on the remote to try to change the channel. *Stupid NCIS. Can't watch that crap.*

I chuckled and turned the TV to a rerun of *House*. After a quick shower, I put on my new clothes then went downstairs to get us some breakfast. I returned a few minutes later with a waffle for Orson and a blueberry muffin for me. We ate quickly then packed up and left for Sarasota.

A fair number of RV parks lay near Sarasota and its coastline. The motor homes in most were shiny and new, owned by retirees pursuing their dreams of cross-country travel.

Happy Acres was not one of those parks. If I imagined every stereotype of a white-trash trailer park, I'd have imagined that place. The bits of yard outside the mobile homes were filled with garbage, broken beer bottles, dilapidated and rusty lawn furniture, and cars up on blocks. Jeff Foxworthy could have gotten enough material for another two albums just by driving down a couple of the dirt roads.

Judith's trailer was no better or worse than her neighbors'. Rust was creeping outward from the corners.

Three sagging wooden steps led to a screen door held on by one hinge.

Wasn't this on Breaking Bad*?*

"Come on, Orson. Just because someone lives in a trailer that doesn't make them a meth head. An alcoholic, sure, but not necessarily a drug addict."

Yeah, right. Like you weren't thinking up redneck jokes.

The stairs groaned under my weight. I banged on the flopping screen door. No one answered.

"She ain't home," a woman called.

I glanced to the right and saw a gaunt woman with a hard face sitting on the porch of the neighboring trailer. I was surprised I hadn't noticed her. "Ma'am?"

"I said, she ain't home," the woman said around the cigarette clenched in her teeth. "Ain't seen her all month."

That was a pretty long beer run. That was also about when Sheila had come down there the first time. "Do you know where she went?"

"No."

"I'm her nephew from Baltimore. No one in the family has seen her in a while, and I was worried."

"You'd think that no-good tramp of a daughter would check up on her. Too busy running around with that creep of a boyfriend."

Nothing like gossip about thankless children to get people talking. "Tell me about it," I said. "She lives an hour away, but do you think she could be bothered? No. Instead, let's have the guy who lives eight hundred miles away drive down here and check in. Not like I don't have to take care of my own mom."

The leathery neighbor nodded. "Kids have no respect. My boy thinks he knows everything. Doesn't know enough to wear a rubber and not to hang around with skanks. Now he's got that to deal with."

I bobbed my head in agreement. "Hey, do you have a

spare key? I really need to let Mom know if her sister's okay."

"No." She waved at the door. "But it's probably not locked."

"Thanks. By the way, that boyfriend of Maddie's, has he been around lately?"

She hacked out a smoker's cough then pulled a paper towel from the pocket of her muumuu. "Hmmm... I don't know." She ground out her cigarette and tapped on the pack for another, but it was empty. "Damn it. I'm outta smokes."

I took the hint. "What do you smoke? Camels?"

"American Spirit. They're all natural." She had a short coughing fit.

I stepped over and handed her a twenty. "Let me buy you a couple packs to thank you for keeping an eye on Aunt Judy's place."

"Well now, that's right neighborly."

"No problem. So this boyfriend of Maddie's, what's he look like?"

"Like some kind of metal punk. Long hair, greasy, weird little pointy beard."

"He have a name?"

"A stupid-sounding one. Jared or something like that."

That was pretty close to Yareth. "Thank you. You've been a big help."

"Whatever. If you find her, tell her I'm still complaining to the park about the noise."

"Noise?"

"The last time her tramp daughter and her creep boyfriend were here, they made a ton of noise. They were playing their stupid music too loud, then they had a big screaming fight. That wasn't the first time, either."

"How long ago was that?"

"About a month, I think. I would have gone over then, but that guy gives me the creeps."

You aren't the only one. "I'll tell her. Thanks."

The woman got up and shuffled down the dirt road, presumably heading to the convenience store across the street from the park. I tried the door to Judith's home. It was unlocked, just as the neighbor had said, so I stepped inside with Orson on my heels.

The front door opened to a large room that served as the living room and kitchen. All the windows were closed, and the air conditioner was off, which made the space stifling. I tried a light switch, but nothing happened. The old refrigerator was humming loudly. The door had been left open, the contents left to rot and stink up the room.

Broken bottles littered the floor, and under the odor of rotting food was the smell of stale alcohol. The coffee table lay in pieces, and the few chairs in the kitchenette had been broken.

Orson whined. *Not good. It feels bad in here.*

I walked down the hall to the small bedroom. The place had been ransacked, the mattress flipped over and all the drawers emptied. The room only had one tiny window, which was just a Plexiglas panel screwed to the frame. Underneath that, an air conditioning unit poked out from the wall.

The only room left to check was the bathroom. I had to push the mattress out of the way to get to the closed door. A horrifying stench wafted out when I opened the door. After seeing the closed shower curtain, I prayed the smell was just the septic tank.

The room was tiny, with barely enough room for a toilet and a tub. I stepped forward and gingerly reached out to pull the curtain aside. My prayer had not been answered.

A woman's body was standing in the tub, arms pulled up and tied to the shower head. The corpse had been there for some time, rotting, and the remaining skin was stretched taut over the bones. There weren't even many insects, since they had gotten what nutrition they could and vacated the premises. A few fat flies crawled along the walls, but that was it. I stretched carefully to open the window above the tub, but the thing was just screwed-on Plexiglas as well.

I could only assume that the body belonged to Judith. I noticed her neck was stuck at an unnatural angle, and a brown stain was splattered on the shower wall in front of her. A black pentagram had been painted on the base of the tub.

Orson whimpered behind me. I felt the urge to join him, but I didn't have time to be squeamish. There might be a clue somewhere.

I guessed that Madison had brought Yareth home to meet her mother. Maybe she had told him what an abusive drunk Mom was, or perhaps he just found out firsthand. I didn't know if he had come there planning to kill her or if it had just been an impulsive act. But the scenario looked as though they had slit her throat as part of some kind of sacrifice. The blood was on top of the pentagram, so the symbol had been drawn before the murder. My dad was an asshole and a drunk, but even he didn't deserve what they had done to that poor woman.

Orson barked. *We have to go. Now!*

"What?"

Don't talk. Move! They're coming!

I ran back into the living room. I pulled the blinds aside a little to peek out the window. A Honda Civic with a MEAN PEOPLE SUCK bumper sticker was heading down the dirt road. Madison was driving, and Yareth was riding shotgun.

TWENTY-SEVEN

THE CAR PULLED TO A stop behind my Ford, effectively blocking me from leaving. I hurried over and locked the deadbolt on the front door, but I doubted that would hold them off for more than a few seconds. They had almost crushed a restaurant the previous night. And they probably wouldn't even need magic to crush the oversized tin can I was standing in.

The pair got out of the car and walked to the foot of the steps. I hadn't seen a back door. They were blocking the only exit. Madison hung onto Yareth's arm as if he were the starting quarterback on the high school football team and she were the lead cheerleader. Yareth cradled the purple stone as if it were the Heisman Trophy. I ducked down, hoping they wouldn't see me. Orson padded over and crouched beside me.

"Hello, Gabriel," Yareth called.

Madison giggled. "Did you say hello to my mommy?"

Well, there was obviously no use in trying to hide the fact that I was there, but I didn't stand up. I wasn't about to give Yareth a visible target. "She didn't deserve that!" I shouted.

"That drunken bitch tried to keep me tied down for years," Madison said with a snarl in her voice.

"She got off easy."

"Black magic's not the way to deal with it." I scanned to see if there was anything I could use as a weapon. Half of all homes in the US were supposed to have guns, but I was apparently in the wrong half. The most deadly things I could see were the scraps of wood from the busted-up kitchenette.

She laughed. "Did that stupid cow Lisa tell you that? You sound just like her whining. My cousin is such a coward. Black magic got rid of one problem for me, and it's going to get rid of a whole lot more."

"Yes," Yareth said. "And right now, today's problem is you. Give me the dog, and you can leave here. No harm will come to you."

Orson whined. *I don't believe him.*

I didn't believe him, either, but even if I had, I wouldn't have traded Orson. I needed to buy some time. I whispered to Orson, "Play along. I'll think of something." I shouted back at Yareth, "How do I know I can trust you?"

Yareth cackled. "You don't."

Madison squealed with laughter. "You have one minute. Then we make things... uncomfortable."

I crawled across the room to search the kitchen. "Orson, do your best to block whatever they try to send us."

You aren't thinking about giving me to them, are you?

I snorted. "As if I could ever make you do anything. Besides, Sheila would kill me if I handed you over to that asshole." I winked at him.

Orson chuffed. *Damn right.*

The range top was spotless, but the microwave was filthy. Even though the late Mrs. Wilkins was likely a TV-dinner-and-takeout kind of gal, I checked the drawers for a cleaver or a butcher knife. No luck. Next, I looked under the sink. I let out a whoosh of breath when I spotted a propane tank.

What are you thinking?

"Nothing good. You remember the window in the bedroom?"

The one that doesn't open? Sure.

146

"When I say the word, run for it."

"Thirty seconds," Yareth yelled.

I gathered up a couple of forks from the silverware drawer and tossed them in the microwave. I called out to my new friends, "You've got to give me a second. The dog has a mind of his own. For some reason, he doesn't like you."

"Well, you've got a second," Yareth responded. "Twenty-five of them, in fact."

I set the timer on the microwave for five minutes. I had to crawl under the sink to disconnect the feeder hose from the propane tank. Once that was done, I opened the spigot. "Orson, move!"

Orson barked in alarm. *Hurry. They're drawing energy.*

I hustled after Orson as he scurried into the bedroom. The small window faced the back of the park, away from Yareth. I just hoped the opening was big enough for me. I grabbed a dresser drawer from the bed and smashed it into the Plexiglas. Orson kept barking at me to hurry. The Plexiglas cracked, and the panel torqued enough that I could push it out.

Yareth shouted from out front, "Time's up!"

Better hurry. I can't hold him off for long.

The roof of the trailer buckled, and rivets began to pop. I picked up Orson and shoved him out the window. I put my hands on the sill, pulled myself up, and squeezed out after him, barely scraping through and getting a nice scratch on my arm. I rolled across the ground to get away from the structure without them seeing me from the front.

Worried we weren't moving fast enough and that the pair might decide to come around back, I snatched up Orson and sprinted around the neighbor's house. The trailers had painted wooden skirts on the bottom that went to the ground, and they were close together, so I didn't think we'd be seen. When I glanced back, the roof and the sides of Judith's trailer rippled like a beer can being flattened. Still holding Orson, I worked my way to the far corner and peeked around the edge of the trailer. Yareth and Madison were standing at the foot of the steps. Yareth seemed focused on his spell casting, but Madison was just gazing dreamily at him.

A crackling noise came from inside Judith's trailer. I stepped back and hunched over Orson to protect him.

Boom!

The explosion shook Muumuu Lady's trailer. I raised my head to look around. I couldn't hear anything over the ringing in my ears.

Orson howled in my head. *Hurt ears!*

"Orson, stop! That hurts." I realized he couldn't hear me, so I patted his back to soothe him.

I leaned forward and peered around the corner. The end of Judith's trailer where the kitchen had been was completely gone. Smoke was pouring out every window. The last hinge on the screen door had given up. A few of the neighbors had roused themselves from their hangovers to come out onto their steps and porches to see what all the noise was. Yareth and Madison had been thrown back a few feet, and both were lying near the car they had arrived in. Madison was holding her head, and I caught a glimpse of crimson between her fingers. Yareth appeared dazed as he just sat there moaning. The purple stone was on the ground a few inches away from him.

"Come on!" I yelled at Orson.

I didn't know if he heard my voice or just figured out what I had said, but either way, he followed me as I sprinted to the convertible. I dumped Orson onto the backseat. As I ran around to the driver's side, a thought hit me. I veered toward Yareth, who still seemed pretty out of it. I bent over and reached for the stone.

"No!" Madison clawed at my leg.

Yareth roused enough to try to pick up the rock. I kicked his arm and snatched up the magic stone. Before he could recover, I ran to the car and hopped behind the wheel without bothering to open the door.

Madison had parked across the road in an attempt to block me in, but the old Honda was no match for my V8. I put the Galaxie in reverse and floored it. My back bumper hit the front panel of the smaller sedan on the driver's side, leaving a nice dent and spinning it out of my way.

I sped out of the park. I didn't let up until we were on the highway and heading north toward Tampa.

Where did you learn how to do that?

"It was in a movie."

We need to watch better films.

TWENTY-EIGHT

AFTER AN HOUR ON THE highway, I hadn't seen any sirens or the red Honda, so I decided it would probably be safe to pull over for a minute. I spotted an outlet mall that wasn't crowded and parked in a far corner of the lot. Orson had hopped into the passenger seat after we left the park, and I had tossed the purple stone into the back.

Orson and I studied the rock warily. I reached out with one finger and poked it. The thing glistened in the sunlight, but other than that I didn't feel any power emanating from it. I touched the ring on Orson's collar. It didn't seem to be drawn toward the rock or anything like that, and Orson wasn't being pulled to it. But that didn't mean much. The only magic I could ever do was pulling a quarter out of Sheila's ear, and that was because she was a forgiving audience.

"What do you think, pal?"

Orson didn't look at me. *I think we should get something to eat.*

"Of course you do. What do you think about the stone?"

I think better on a full stomach.

"You're stalling."

Yes, but I'm still hungry.

"What's the matter? You've been using the small stone in that ring for a couple of days." I gestured at the big rock. "That's just a bigger version."

That's like saying a jumbo jet is a bigger version of a paper airplane.

I grabbed his collar and tugged on it until he faced me. "You had the ring and you were able to touch Sheila. If you have the rock—"

You don't understand. Everyone who knew him said that Yareth was a chump. Then he got this rock, and now he can crush houses.

"Right, so use it to find Mama."

Orson growled. *It's not that easy. What if the rock is what made Yareth go crazy? What if he tainted the power of the stone with his energy? What happens if it makes me do things I don't want to?*

"Orson, you're not bad. We're trying to find Sheila, who was hiding from this guy. You aren't using this for evil or to hurt anyone."

I know.

"If I could do it myself, I would." I didn't know if I would use it to reach Sheila, or if I would just use it to shake Yareth around until he told me where she was. Maybe Orson had a point.

I'm still worried. I don't want to do something that would make it worse.

"Me either." I stared at the rock for a few seconds. "How about a nice hamburger? Then you take a crack at it."

Orson whined but nodded. *And ice cream?*

"You got it."

I started the car and pulled back onto the highway. We stopped at a McDonald's a few miles down the road. I stashed the purple rock in the trunk. I didn't think anyone would steal it, but there was no sense in leaving it out for the world to see. Well, and carrying it into the restaurant would have made us look pretty strange.

The trailer park showdown had left me on edge, and I wasn't hungry. Orson had no such problem. I ordered a quarter pounder meal and an ice cream cone, which he devoured. After Orson ate, I let him blow off some steam in the ball pit. The three kids in there with him shrieked with laughter. Their parents paid no attention, and fortunately, the staff didn't seem to care.

I picked at Orson's leftover fries while I tried to think. Yareth and Madison had shown up a bit too quickly for my taste. Even if they had set up some kind of alarm in the trailer or paid off Muumuu Lady to call when I arrived, they would never have gotten there that fast. Also, the neighbors seemed to have no love for the pair.

I didn't get how they could have known we were going to be there at that particular time. I hadn't even known Madison's mom existed, let alone that I would be visiting her, until the night before when I had talked to Lisa. I tried to squelch the nagging feeling that she had ratted us out. I believed she wanted to help. And even if she had told the coven about my call, I doubted she would have mentioned that I was going to see Madison's mother. Plus, the coven might not be willing to help me, but they had no reason to try to stop me from finding Sheila, at least none that I was aware of.

Then I remembered something Lisa had said. *Madison visited me in New York. She and Sheila helped me move into my new place.*

Madison had visited Lisa in her new place. Madison had helped Lisa move in. Madison was a young witch who wanted to learn more from her cousin. Madison had access to Lisa's phone and could have bugged it. That had to be it. It would explain why she was so quick to find us, even though Wendy smashed that tracker.

There were a hundred websites out there that would sell you spy gear and phone bugs to keep track of wayward spouses and shady nannies. Madison had tried to kill me once and steal Orson a couple times. Would it be so hard to imagine her bugging someone's phone?

I beckoned to Orson. He bounded up to me and drooled

out three red and blue plastic balls on my feet, covered in spit. *I brought you a present.*

"Do you know where those balls have been?"

Don't worry. They're cleaner now.

"Come on. I've got an idea."

When we got back to the car, Orson didn't seem any more enthusiastic about touching the big stone than he had before he'd eaten, and since the adrenaline of playing out a live-action Jason Bourne film had worn off, I was starting to feel a little less gung-ho about the whole thing myself. The last time Orson had felt Sheila, we'd been in Orlando, so it made the most sense to head there before he tried again. Having suitably convinced myself, I keyed the ignition and drove out of the McDonald's parking lot.

We arrived in Orlando late that afternoon. I pulled into the lot of a Target and parked in a corner at the back of the building. I retrieved the stone from the trunk and placed it on the seat in front of Orson. He eyed it the way he would a piece of broccoli.

I waved at the rock. "Go on." When he didn't move, I added, "You know it's still our best shot."

He grunted and whined. *I know.*

He pawed at the stone for a second. He put his head down on it, closed his eyes, and started to hum. Or the stone started to hum. Or maybe they both did. It was hard to tell. The car began to shudder. Orson opened his eyes, and they glowed purple. He yelped and fell backward against the seat, his back paws knocking the rock to the floor. The car stopped shaking.

Panting heavily, Orson looked over at me. *She's here.*

"Orlando?"

Closer.

"Where?"

Orson stood up on the seat and put his paws on the dash. *There.*

We had parked facing away from the Target, pointed

toward the busy road. Across the street was an abandoned resort development with five buildings, each one painted a different garish color: yellow, aqua, green, pink, and purple. The area looked as if Miami Vice had puked all over it. Boards had been used to cover the ground floor doors and windows. A chain link fence surrounded the entire complex.

"Those buildings?"

Yes. Don't ask which one. Can't tell more than that.

The Target was less than a mile from the last hotel we'd stayed at. "We were this close the whole time?"

She hides herself well. It's only because we were so close I could feel her. Orson wheezed and dropped back into the seat.

"Are you okay to walk?"

Give me a minute.

"Come on! If she's there, we're going to find her."

He shook his body vigorously. We could be minutes away from seeing Sheila for the first time in weeks, and he could barely rouse himself. That stone must have done a number on him. I got out and went around to his side to open the passenger door. He hopped out and almost fell over when he hit the ground. I took the ring off his collar in case that was messing him up, too.

I scooped up the stone from the passenger seat. I wasn't going leave it in the car like at the restaurant, but carrying it around in the open would still draw too much attention. I fished around in the backseat and plucked out the plastic Wal-Mart shopping bag that had my dirty clothes in it. I wrapped the rock in a couple of my dirty T-shirts and put it back in the bag to take with us.

Across the six-lane street, the driveway to the complex was gated and secured by a chain with a No Trespassing sign prominently displayed. There were some tire ruts, but it was hard to tell how recent they were. They were most likely left by the property agent, but they could have been made by a horde of magic cultists, I supposed. From a distance, the chain seemed sturdy. I could have driven the car through it, but I definitely didn't need anyone calling the police. And if Sheila was hiding in there, I didn't want to scare her.

I was tempted to dart through a break in the traffic, but Orson was still dazed from touching the stone. We waited and crossed with the light. I tried to act casual, just a man and his dog going for a stroll in an abandoned resort development with a giant magic stone mixed in with laundry.

We hiked through the scrub grass at the edge of the road, checking for a break in the fence. Eventually, we were able to turn away from the street and head toward what was either a small lake or a large pond. The fence ran down to the beach... well, most of the way. Apparently, the low-bid contractor had put the fence up at high tide. Since it was low tide, we were able to step around it easily. We didn't even get our feet wet.

I checked on Orson and noticed that he was struggling with walking through the sand. "Are you okay?"

Yeah. Kind of.

I picked him up. His tummy moved in and out with his shallow breathing. I felt really bad about making him touch that rock. "I'm sorry."

Stop it. I'm not dying. That stone was just exhausting.

I patted his head. "Mama's going to kiss it and make it better."

We approached the back of the complex. The five buildings lay in a semicircle around the beach, each one facing the water. We moved in and stood in the center of the communal patio.

"Any idea which one?"

No. I can't feel anything. I'm sorry. So tired.

None of the boards over the doors seemed to have been dislodged or moved. I decided to just work my way through the buildings one by one. The aqua house on the left was the closest, and it was as good a place as any to start.

"Do you want to wait here?"

No. I need to help.

I walked slowly so Orson could keep up. Up close, I could see that the plywood over the doorway had been secured with a bit of overkill. At least a dozen nails had been used. The layer of dust on the steps was untouched.

"Not this one. Let's check the yellow."

We trudged to the neighboring house on the right. The bright, sunshiny house was the same.

I sighed. "Okay. On to the next."

Orson gave a doggie nod. *I like purple.*

Purple like the stone. Maybe it was more than a coincidence.

At the purple house, the door was boarded up like the rest, but one of the windows had a board missing, leaving half of it uncovered. I looked around and spotted the missing board to the side of the steps. I bent over and picked it up.

"Well, someone has been here, I think." Using the broken board, I pried loose the remaining plywood.

The window wasn't large, but I could fit through the opening. I stuck my head in and looked around to make sure no magic users were lying in wait, but the room looked empty. I picked up Orson and set him on the floor inside, then I squeezed in after him. If crawling through windows was going to be a new hobby of mine, I really needed to cut down on the cheeseburgers.

The light from the window didn't reach very far. There was no furniture or anything to show that anyone had ever lived there. The floor was covered by a thick carpet, and the humidity had given it a moldy odor.

We checked through the six rooms on the downstairs floor. All of them emptied into a main dining area. Nothing.

Upstairs. Orson had felt something. Maybe he was

perking up a little. He nodded to a spiral staircase at the back of the kitchen. I ran up the stairs with Orson on my heels.

TWENTY-NINE

THE STAIRWAY ENDED AT THE front of a large den. In the middle of the room, Sheila was sitting cross-legged on the floor with her back to us. She had on one of her favorite sundresses. Normally, the outfit clung to her body in all the right places, but at the moment, it looked damp and dirty pooled around her.

I froze. I hadn't seen her in two weeks, and she was finally right in front of me.

Orson barked and whined, "Mama."

A second later, I remembered how to move and ran over to her. "Sheila! Oh, thank God! Sheila!" I threw my arms around her.

Orson jumped up to lick her.

She was clammy and moist. And she didn't hug back.

Orson whined and paced back and forth in front of her. *Gabriel...*

I tried to spin her around, but she didn't budge. She seemed glued to the floor. I slid around in front of her. Her eyes were shut, and her hands rested on her knees. Her breathing was shallow.

"Sheila? Sheila!" I shook her gently.

Stop! Don't hurt her!

Her face was thinner than it had been just two weeks ago, but she didn't seem physically injured.

"What's wrong? Why isn't she answering?"

Orson closed his eyes and put his head against her hand. *She's here, but she's not.*

I wanted to pull my hair out. "What the hell are you talking about?"

Her spirit... her soul... it's gone.

"Gone? Gone where?"

Orson growled. *I don't know! You think I'm trying to hide her?*

I strode around the room, rubbing my face. After all that time, all that traveling, facing Yareth and his gang... after all we had been through, we finally found her, but she was still lost. "What can we do?"

I don't know! I don't know! Orson wailed and howled. He licked Sheila's cheek then dropped down to lie in front of her.

I wanted to howl too. I was ready to punch a hole in the moldy wall of that half-built hotel. Then I remembered what Sheila was always telling me to try to do when I got angry. *Relax. Focus. Breathe.* I grabbed Orson and hugged him. "Come on, buddy. Calm down."

I kept my breathing deep and even as I willed him to stop whining and howling. After a minute, his body relaxed in my arms.

"This isn't going to help her. We've got to keep our heads."

Mama...

"I know." I closed my eyes and squeezed Orson tighter. I counted my inhalations, slowing my breathing. I felt my heart rate drop. Sheila always said, "When you meditate, breathe out the anger, breathe out the frustration..."

My eyes sprang open. I put Orson down.

What?

"I think I have an idea."

I took the stone out of the bag and put it on the floor between Sheila and me. I nudged it closer to her until it was touching her hand. I put one of my hands on the rock and the other on her cheek. Eying the stone warily, Orson came over and rested his head on her knee.

"Sheila always meditates to think through problems. Yareth is a pretty big problem. Maybe she's in a deep trance."

Never gone so far before.

"Well, then it's a good thing both her boys are here with a giant magic rock."

Orson peered up at me with those big, sad eyes.

"When Yareth's group attacked Wendy, they combined their powers by touching the rock. If we all touch it together, maybe you and I can get through to her."

Orson whined. *I don't want to touch it again.*

"I don't have a better idea. I wouldn't ask if it wasn't for her."

He gave a dog's version of a resigned shrug, lowering his head and tail. *Then let's get to it.* He scooted around and put his paw on the stone.

I put my hand on top of his paw. "Do you know what you're doing?"

Not really. I'm going to try and call her like I do. Just grab on, and maybe we can put our strength together. Orson closed his eyes.

I closed mine too. I tried to focus on nothing except my breathing and heartbeat. Orson was more... present than usual, as if the stone made him that much more vibrant. I wasn't really sure what our little plan was going to do. Orson had magic, and Sheila had magic. I had none. I just loved her. I hoped that would count for something.

Orson chuffed. I tried to match his breathing and focus on slowing my heart rate. I cleared my head and thought only of Sheila. I tried to send my love to her. I pictured her laughing, how her hair sparkled in the sunlight. I held on to an image of her smile from the last time I'd seen her, when the sun had framed her in the mist from a fountain, giving her a halo.

The traffic from the busy highway faded into the background. I no longer felt the humidity of the late afternoon or the sweat pooling on my skin. Heat emanated from the stone, but that faded away as well. There was nothing but the void. And Orson and I were the void. I could see nothing, but I could feel his presence, like a cloud of fur and drool, which was oddly reassuring. I opened myself up, every nerve ending ready and waiting for contact.

Orson's wails were all around me. *Mama... Mama...*

Sheila...

No response.

Mama...

Sheila...

Gabriel, I'm here.

A wave of purple washed over me, and Sheila's sweet voice embraced me. I could feel the happy yip from Orson.

It was her. I couldn't see her, but it was definitely her. It took all my will to keep my heart from racing. *Where are you?*

I'm right here.

Orson whined. *Mama, where? We can't see you!*

Shush, baby. I'm still here. Her voice purred in my brain.

I tried to reach out to her. *Sheila, come back to us. We found what you were trying to get. We can go back now.*

What? She sounded worried.

I responded, *The rock. We found the purple rock. We took it from Yareth.*

The purple light changed to a darker shade as Sheila answered, *You have the rock?*

Yes! I answered. *It's how we can reach you now. Come back to us.*

It's not safe. You're in danger.

I know. They tried to take Orson.

Why did you come down? I knew this would happen. She sounded upset.

What should we have done? Leave you alone down here? We were scared and worried!

I'm sorry.

Why didn't you tell us what was happening? Why did you shut us out?

Why, Mama? Orson's whine seemed to be everywhere.

I couldn't risk them finding you! They seemed to know what I was going to do!

But you had to know we would have tried to find you.

Yes.

And we would follow the same trail you did. I think they bugged Lisa's phone. That's how they found you. And how they found us.

Madison. That bitch. Her anger came with a pulse of purple light so dark it was almost black.

I've never heard you swear before.

Her surprised laughter felt like a summer mist on my face. *Well, you might hear it a lot more.*

Mama, come out. Orson's chuffing was hot and eager.

All right. I'm coming. I need to scratch your head in person.

I relaxed. I could hear the horns and sirens outside again as I came around. It had gotten dark. I wondered how long that conversation had taken. Orson was twitching, then he cried and barked.

"What's wrong?" I asked him.

He pawed the floor then licked Sheila's face. She didn't move.

"Orson, what happened? Where's Sheila?"

She's stuck. She can't get back. She's trapped!

Not knowing what else to do, I grabbed her shoulders and shook her. I noticed that her neck was bare and remembered the necklace Yareth had left for me. A sick feeling settled in the pit of my stomach.

THIRTY

"**Y**ARETH. IT MUST HAVE BEEN him!"

Sheila sat there, unmoving and unresponsive. "What did he do?"

There's some kind of block. Mama can't get back.

I massaged my temples and tried to take deep breaths, but I wasn't winning the battle with my anger. "Goddamn it!"

Yareth was behind her condition. He was somehow keeping her trapped. He must have found her and used that rock to keep her in a trance. Then he took her necklace to show me that he had her.

"Why didn't she follow us out?"

I thought she could. That's kind of what we were trying to do. But we weren't strong enough to pull her through.

I really needed to throw something. Unfortunately, there was no furniture in the unfinished resort. I took the disposable cell phone out of my pocket and disposed of it—*loudly*—against the far wall. That wasn't enough.

When I was a kid and I couldn't take my dad's drunkenness and my mother's crying and my own weakness anymore, I would run into the woods behind our house. I would run and run until I couldn't run anymore, then I would collapse on the ground and scream. I would scream out all of my frustration until my throat was raw. After that, I would slump back home and try to sneak into my room without being seen.

So I screamed. I screamed and yelled and punched the wall.

Orson cowered and covered his head. *Stop!*

I stopped and bent over at the waist. I was winded, and my knuckles were throbbing. The wall was surprisingly tough.

Do you feel better?

"A little."

Good. Now cut it out. This isn't helping Mama.

"I know. I just feel so helpless. This is all I can do."

You are not helpless. We wouldn't be here if it weren't for you. I wouldn't, that's for sure.

"How did Yareth trap her?"

Maybe he had the whole gang together to cast something. Strength in numbers.

Right. Numbers. And I knew where we could find one more to help us.

The nice thing about driving with a magic dog that could scramble radar guns was that it certainly cut down on travel time in an emergency. We got to Lakeland just after ten o'clock.

I hadn't wanted to leave Sheila alone in that deserted hotel, but I couldn't move her. I had tried to roll her off her spot, but she wouldn't budge. I didn't know whether that was because of the trance or because of something Yareth had done. Either way, it couldn't be helped, so I had kissed her cheek and promised to be back soon. I doubted she heard me, though.

I screeched to a stop in front of The Sand Witch. A big sign out front told the public: Open During Renovations. At the bottom was written Excuse Our Mess! The place had closed a few hours ago, so we headed around back to the door that I hoped led to Wendy's apartment.

I knocked loudly. Orson growled, and I wondered why.

But before I could ask him, I got my answer. The window shade rose, and Wendy stood in the window with a shotgun pointed at my head.

I threw my hands up in the air. "Don't shoot! It's me and Orson!"

She lowered the shotgun. "Sorry about that." She disappeared for a minute, and I heard her disengaging a security chain. She opened the door and waved us in. "I'm still a little on edge from the other night."

"I couldn't tell. I heard most witches don't like guns."

"Yeah, well, most witches don't get their roofs torn half off by a bunch of magic bastards, either. I figure if they won't respect my mystic arts, maybe something more mundane like Dad's twelve gauge will do."

She wasn't getting any argument from me. I was quickly changing my personal stance on guns. After a few more days of dealing with Yareth, I'd be a walking NRA ad.

"What brings you here so late?" she asked.

"Sorry to be back so soon, but we need your help."

"Is it Yareth again? Because I would love to go a few more rounds with him and take the insurance deductible out of his hide."

"Kind of. We found Sheila."

She put a hand over her heart. "Thank goodness! Is she all right?"

I rubbed the bridge of my nose. "Sort of." I didn't know quite how to explain it. "You know, Orson can probably tell you faster."

Orson chuffed.

Wendy looked down at him and met his gaze. Her eyes grew wider and wider. A few seconds later, she said, "That *bastard!*"

I nodded. "Orson and I aren't strong enough to guide her back. Can you help?"

"Of course. You kept my shop from being destroyed.

It's the least I can do. I only hope I'm strong enough to help."

We piled into the car. Wendy brought along the shotgun. I didn't complain.

THIRTY-ONE

W HEN WE ARRIVED AT THE intersection where the garish resort was located, I started to turn into the Target lot again.

Orson barked urgently. *Look.* He was standing on the seat, staring out the window.

I looked in that direction. The gate to the resort was partway open. "It's probably nothing. Maybe it was just the security company making nightly rounds."

Wendy raised one eyebrow at me. "You really believe that?"

"No." Instead of turning left into the parking lot, I ignored the honking horns of my fellow motorists and cut across three lanes of traffic. I barreled into the gate, forcing it open the rest of the way. If Yareth was there, I didn't see much point in trying to be subtle. And if he was with Sheila, I wasn't going to waste any time.

Orson was growling. Wendy stroked his neck.

"Do you feel him?" I asked.

Yes.

The driveway ended at the common patio area. A familiar Honda Civic with some lovely new dents was parked in front of the purple house. Yareth must have had some magic trigger or ward we tripped when we came in, and Orson had been too exhausted to notice.

We got out of the car and walked to the porch. The board that had been over the doorway was gone, and the door was wide open. A faint glow emanated from the entryway. Since there was no power, I hoped the light was from the streetlights around front shining through the upstairs windows and not from a bunch of witches and warlocks making fireballs. The whole place was eerily silent.

"Wendy, give me the gun."

"What?"

"I know guns. I don't know how this stone works, but it's magical. You and Orson will have a much better chance at using it against Yareth than I will. I love her desperately, but I don't know how all this is supposed to work."

Wendy handed me the shotgun. "Love is powerful, and it's the most basic, primal magic of all. Don't discount it so easily."

I gave her the stone. She tried to hide her reaction, but I could see her shiver when she touched it.

"Orson, they're upstairs, aren't they?" I asked.

Yes.

"Can you tell how many?"

Orson closed his eyes. *I can tell they're there, but he's trying to block me. There are at least three. Maybe four. And Mama.*

I could almost feel Yareth's eyes on me, even though all the windows were covered. "Okay, you two stay down here."

What?

Wendy put a hand on my arm. "Don't be stupid!"

I shook her off. "Yareth wants the stone, and he wants Orson. I'm not going to waltz up there with both of those. You two try to guide Sheila back while I see what's going on."

I don't like this. It's going to be harder if we can't touch Mama.

"I don't like it, either, but I like the idea of them sitting up there with Sheila even less. There's only one car here, so you're right, Orson. There can't be more than four up there."

Wendy took my hand and placed it on the rock, then she grabbed Orson by the scruff of his neck. She stared at me intently. "Look at me."

"What?"

"Just do it."

I gazed into Wendy's eyes. They were hazel, flecked with amber and gold.

"Now," she murmured, "keep your mind open. We'll try to help Sheila, but we'll keep an eye open for you. If you get into trouble, we'll know."

I nodded. I didn't think there was any point in arguing with them about staying out of my head.

Wendy spoke in my mind. *Go get her.*

Orson chimed in, *Yeah, go save Mama.*

Having them with me was warm and comforting. I nodded, hoping I came off more confident than I felt. I approached the door.

THIRTY-TWO

T HE AIR WAS STILL HUMID and moist, even though the sun had set hours ago. The traffic noise from the road seemed to fade away to a faint drone. Or maybe that was the mosquitoes. I slapped one away from the back of my neck.

The stairway hadn't changed since that afternoon, but it seemed much more ominous, and not just because of the dim light. I pumped the shotgun and started up the stairs.

Sheila was right where we had left her. Unfortunately, she had new companions. Madison and Yareth flanked Sheila. In front of them was a new guy, another kid they might have found in the Manic Panic aisle. Good old Morty stood off to my left. I almost smiled. Morty noticed that and winced. He had probably just about had his fill of the lifestyle of a dark wizard.

I mentally asked Wendy and Orson, *Are you seeing this?*

Wendy responded, *Yes.*

Have you found Sheila?

We've made contact, but we're still having trouble getting her back.

Sheila remained motionless. She didn't seem to be reacting to anything Wendy and Orson were doing.

Stall for time, Wendy said. *We'll keep at it.*

I raised the shotgun. "Hey, everybody. Why don't you all

just step away from the lady and go home before someone gets hurt?"

Yareth laughed. "You're in no position to give orders." He flicked his wrist, and a knife popped out of his sleeve, a dagger with a six-inch blade and a jeweled hilt. He placed it at the base of Sheila's neck. "Look. It's been a long day, and you have proven to be quite a nuisance. But I'll make this easy for you. Give me the stone and the dog, and you can take her away."

My finger tensed on the shotgun trigger. Yareth was about fifteen feet away and way too close to Sheila. There was no way to shoot him without hitting her. I would have been better off reversing the gun and using it as a club.

"Well, what's your decision?" He poked the knife into the soft spot under her chin, drawing a trickle of blood.

I told myself to stay calm, focus, and breathe. I needed to stall so Orson and Wendy could have more time to get to Sheila. "Orson won't go with you. You should know that. And what do you want with him anyway?"

Madison sneered. "That dog is the most powerful familiar I've ever seen. He's wasting his time with this useless bitch." She thumped Sheila's shoulder. "He'd be much better off with a powerful man like Yareth who can use him to his full potential."

Yareth puffed out his chest. Peacocks everywhere would have told him to tone it down.

I narrowed my eyes. "You stupid cow. I don't know anything about magic, but even I know that's not how it works." I took a step closer to the group.

Her face reddened. "One more step, and he'll..."

I smirked with a bravado I didn't feel. "He'll what? Kill her? If he does that, then what's to stop me from shooting you morons?"

Morty tried to act brave. "There are four of us. You can't shoot us all."

I nodded. "You're right. But if you hurt her, you'd better pray I shoot you first."

Morty stepped back. He'd run out of courage for the night, and he was probably out of clean underwear. Yareth was staring at me, the knife still in place.

Madison said, "Don't push us. Do you really want to test us?"

We were stuck in a standoff. Part of me wanted to just give them the stone, but I feared we would need it to get Sheila back. Also, Yareth wanted Orson, and I wouldn't even dream of making that trade.

I hadn't seen any hint from Sheila that what Wendy and Orson were doing was working. *Wendy, Orson, help me out here.*

Wendy answered, *It's hard. We're almost there, but we need more power. Is there any way we could touch her?*

Not a chance.

Then we need your help. Come back downstairs.

I glared at Yareth. "Okay. You win." I backed toward the stairs. "You stay here, and I'll go down and get Orson and the stone." I wiggled the shotgun. "Anyone follows me, the deal's off. It's going to be hard enough to get the dog to come up with me without any of you lurking behind me."

I inched down the stairs backward, keeping the weapon trained on the opening at the top. The last thing I saw as I got below floor level was Madison smirking.

THIRTY-THREE

W HEN I STEPPED OUTSIDE, WENDY and Orson were on the porch, both touching the stone. Their eyes were closed. I hurried over and knelt next to them. I put one hand over Orson's paw and let my fingers drape over it so they made contact with the stone. I placed my other hand over Wendy's in the same manner.

The same falling sensation came over me, then I was surrounded by blackness. I could sense Wendy and Orson.

After a moment, I saw Sheila. Her form shimmered, going in and out of focus. She smiled at me, and my heart melted. I reached out with ethereal arms and tried to hold her, but my hands closed around empty space. *Sheila?*

I'm here, she said.

You have to come back.

I'm trying, but I can't.

Wendy sent out a thought. *The shield is cracking, but it's still strong. Even with the stone, I can't break through. If I could touch her, it would help.*

I shook my head. *They aren't going to let you anywhere near her.*

Gabriel, can you get close to me? Sheila asked. *Can you touch me?*

I had an idea. I didn't know if it would be possible or even if it could work, but we had to try. *Wendy, if I had contact with the stone and Orson, then I touched her, could that work?*

Maybe. But then you'd have the same problem as the last time. She couldn't break through before with just you and Orson helping.

What if she wasn't trying to break through from the void? What if she tried to get back into her body through me?

Orson let out a mental whine.

Sheila gasped. *No! You can't do that! If I got stuck inside you, then it would hurt us both! Your mind can't handle two separate entities for long. It could give you a stroke or an aneurism!*

Wendy spoke up. *It might work, but it's risky. If you can't get her back in, she could be trapped inside you.*

I didn't care. *I don't think we have a lot of options. They have a knife to her neck up there. If I don't give them Orson and the stone, they'll kill her. If I do give them Orson and the stone, they'll leave, and I don't think they'll be good sports and take away the block they put on Sheila. We have to try.*

Silence reigned for a moment. Then I felt reluctant sighs from each of them.

All right, Sheila said. *I'll do it. This won't be comfortable for either of us. But you need to prepare yourself. The big thing is for you to relax and clear your mind.*

I closed my eyes. Remembering all the things Sheila had taught me about meditation—*breathe, focus*—I cleared all thoughts from my head. Sheila's presence was all around me. I could almost feel her soft touch, her gentle breath on my cheek, the feathery brush of her long hair.

I love you.

I love you, too.

Suddenly, I felt as if I had been dropped from a three-story building. Once that plummeting sensation had passed, I landed back in my body with a thud.

I opened my eyes. I tried to take a step, but I almost

fell over. I lurched against the wall. Sheila was in my head and throwing me off balance.

Careful, honey.

"Thanks, babe. Doin' my best."

Orson shook his head. *This better work.*

Wendy grabbed my shoulder. "Make sure you touch her body, Orson, and the stone. You'll have to be in contact with them all at the same time."

I nodded. "Come on, Orson. Let's do this."

Orson growled. *I am not going with those guys.*

"You won't. Once we sort this out, run downstairs to Wendy and get out. Don't let him touch you."

Sheila was almost growling as well. *If they harm my baby...*

"Worry about yourself. They have a knife under your chin. If this works, as soon as you're back in your body, you'll need to try to get away from it. Your best bet is probably to roll backward. You'll have the element of surprise."

I hope so. My body may be pretty stiff.

"I'll be right here." I imagined stroking her cheek. I hoped she could feel it.

Okay. I'm ready.

I picked up the shotgun with my right hand and the stone with my left. We went back into the condo and headed up the stairs. I had to move slowly to ensure I would stay on my feet. Hopefully, Yareth would think I was just reluctant. When we reached the top, I was relieved to see that the tableau hadn't changed.

Sheila gasped in my head. *I'm bleeding.* She had seen the trickle of blood Yareth had left.

It's okay, I told her. *Keep cool. We'll get out of this.*

I held up the stone. "Okay, I've got them." I nudged Orson with my foot. He growled but scooted forward a few inches.

Yareth pointed at me. "Drop the gun!"

I frowned. "You think I trust you enough to do that?"

"No closer!" Yareth motioned to Morty. "Hand over the stone. We'll take the dog and be on our way."

Morty took a step toward Orson, who snarled and snapped at him. Morty jumped away.

I shook my head. "No way. Orson's not going to go with you until he's sure his mama's all right."

"Fine," Yareth said. "Roll the stone to me, and we'll let him check her out."

"There is no way I'm letting you anywhere near this stone until I'm sure she's okay. Orson and I are going to go over there and make sure she's all right. Then, and only then, do you get the stone."

"And the dog," Yareth added.

"Yeah."

"Get rid of the gun." He poked the knife into Sheila's chin. "Remember, you aren't the one to make demands."

I could feel Sheila's shock become anger. *Calm down, babe.* Not willing to turn my back on Yareth and his gang, I knelt and put the shotgun on the floor behind me, pointing down the staircase. As I stood again, I used my foot to scoot the gun backward until it started a slow slide down the stairs. The trigger required a heavy finger, so I was fairly certain it wouldn't go off from the jolting as it slid over the steps. Once I heard it thunk to a stop, I stepped forward, Orson inching ahead of me.

"Get that fucking knife out of the way," I told Yareth. "And step away from her."

Sneering, Yareth lowered the knife and moved back. He gestured at Madison, and she went over to stand by the window.

Everybody ready? I asked.

Yes, Sheila responded, *but be careful.*

Orson grunted and trotted over to her. Keeping an eye on Yareth, I closed the distance and went down on one knee in front of Sheila. Orson stretched his neck and sniffed at her face.

"Satisfied?" Yareth asked impatiently.

I glanced up at him. "No. She's not moving. What did you do to her?" I played it up by waving my hand in front of her face.

"She'll be fine as soon as I get what I want," he answered.

"Orson needs to say goodbye to her. He won't go without that."

"Fine. Get it over with."

Orson climbed onto Sheila's lap, stretched up, and licked her face. I laid the stone on her left knee, hoping Orson's and my bodies were blocking the view. Orson moved a paw onto the stone, and I placed my left hand over it with my fingers draped and touching the rock. With my right hand, I reached up and touched Sheila's face. Orson howled in my head, and the stone glowed in my peripheral vision as I stared at Sheila, willing her to open her eyes.

My left hand was getting hot. I felt lightheaded as Sheila's consciousness left mine, and I closed my eyes. I could faintly hear Madison and Yareth shouting. Hands were trying to pull the stone away. Someone screamed, then I smelled something burning. A kick to my hand broke my contact with the stone.

I gasped and opened my eyes. Madison was rolling around on the floor, shaking her hands. They were red and smoldering. Yareth went over to check on her. She'd managed to kick the stone a few feet away. Morty and the other guy had Orson backed into a corner. Orson was growling and yapping.

I stared at Sheila. *Come on...*

Her eyelids fluttered. Then they opened a little.

Thank you. Oh God, Goddess, thank you.

Yareth lurched over to us. He held up the dagger. "What have you done to the stone?"

"Nothing compared to what I'm going to do to yours." I reared back and kicked up at his groin.

Yareth squeaked and grabbed his crotch. Almost in slow motion, he slid down to the floor.

I got to my feet, but I was still a bit shaky. I lurched over to Sheila. "Sheila, honey, are you okay?"

"Yeah... I think so..." Her voice was dry and creaky.

"Can you move?"

She moaned. "I don't know."

"We have to get out of here." I looked around frantically. "Orson!"

Orson was still trying to evade Morty and his friend. The new kid got his hand too close, and Orson bit hard. The guy screamed and snatched his hand back. Orson took the opportunity to sprint through his legs and head for us.

I pulled Sheila to her feet, and we limped to the stairs. I was basically dragging her. Orson whimpered, nudging her along.

As we reached the top step, someone shouted, "Stop right there!"

I looked over my shoulder. Morty was aiming a pink handgun at my back. *Great.* He had been home to see Mom. The gun was a .22 caliber, which didn't have a lot of stopping power, but the bullet could rattle around in a person's skull.

I maneuvered Sheila so that she stood behind me. "Morty, stop this. Haven't you been through enough?"

"Fuck you. I don't care what Yareth says. This is payback for the alligators and the dinosaurs." He squeezed the trigger.

I stood my ground, determined to protect Sheila.

Bang!

The deafening boom had been way too loud for the Hello-Kitty popgun. Morty screamed and dropped to the floor. I turned and saw Wendy standing beside me. She held the shotgun.

Morty was rolling around on the floor, screaming and clawing at his eyes. He was hurt but alive. I was confused. A shotgun blast that close should have torn him in half and left a pulpy mess.

Wendy winked and nodded at the gun. "Rock salt. It scares away prowlers and vandals."

"Rock salt?" I repeated. "Rock salt!"

She shrugged. "I don't want to kill anyone. We have to go. That won't hold him long."

Even as she spoke, Yareth crawled to his feet and lunged at us. Wendy fired, emptying the other barrel, and he dove for cover. Morty blindly rolled a little too close, so I kicked him. He rocked away with a whimper.

We hurried down the steps. At the bottom, I looked up and saw Madison and the new guy staring down at me, but they didn't seem to make a move to follow. We hurried outside, and I closed the front door behind us, figuring that might at least slow them down a second or two.

I helped Sheila into the back seat, and Orson leapt in to sit next to her. Wendy took the passenger seat, and I got behind the wheel. As I pulled onto the driveway, I noticed that Wendy had been busy. All four tires on Madison's Honda were flat.

I fishtailed onto the main road and sped away. It wasn't until we were in the next county that I remembered that I had left the stone in the resort.

THIRTY-FOUR

W E RODE DOWN 192 FOR almost an hour, no one saying much. We left the tourist strips and shopping malls and got into the marshy interior. We passed signs for Cat Lake and Alligator Lake. Orson snuffled next to Sheila.

I didn't want to drive too far with Sheila in such a bad condition. She needed somewhere to rest and recover. Just after midnight, I spotted a small roadside motel. The place was a seedy dive. The clerk took cash and didn't even ask for a credit card.

With Wendy's help, I got Sheila into the room and onto the bed. Her breathing was raspy, and she seemed really out of it.

"Get her some water," Wendy said. "Her body shut down while she was in that trance. She's dehydrated. God knows how long she was in that room with the heat and humidity."

I found a couple of plastic cups by the sink. I took the plastic wrapper off one and filled it with water that smelled like rotten eggs because of too much sulfur from the surrounding marshes. I wet a washcloth and took that and the cup over to the bed. I put the cloth on her head and tried to sit her up a little on the pillows. I tipped the cup to her lips and let some water dribble into her mouth. She coughed but managed to swallow some.

"I'll get some ice." I grabbed the cracked plastic bucket and went out to find a machine.

The air outside was heavy and thick. The buzzing of insects was almost as loud as the noise from the occasional car passing on the road. A bug zapper overhead was working overtime. I spotted the ice machine at the end of the building.

Placing the bucket under the spout, I pressed the button on the front. The machine whirred and emitted a clinking noise, but no ice came out. I held the button down, and for the first time all day, I paused to think.

Sheila, Orson, and I were finally back together. We needed to head home as soon as she felt up to it and get as far away as possible from crazy magic people. I knew I should be happy, but I was just drained. I wanted to sleep for a week and forget I ever knew about things like magic stones, warlocks, and witches.

The girl I was with before Sheila was named Rebecca. She was a lawyer who did contracts and corporate work. She liked to go to Broadway shows and watch *Grey's Anatomy* when she had any free time outside of her seventy-hour work week. She was hardworking, predictable, and dull. There was no chance I would have ever had to chase her down the coast to save her from wizards and crazy trailer-park witches. She was also allergic to dogs. I didn't think she cared much one way or the other when we broke up. I was a box to check off. *Loft? Check. Junior partner? Check. Boyfriend? Check.*

So I could put up with the occasional vengeance-crazed warlock if Sheila was the reward. Our first date after Orson mushed us together was not what anyone would call a success. I had bought movie tickets online, but our subway got stuck for half an hour, and the movie was half over by the time we got there. The teenager at the ticket booth couldn't change our ticket, since it was the last show of the day. I was embarrassed. I hadn't been so flustered in front of a girl since I was fourteen. I was just about to swear at the poor teenager and slam my fist on the counter or do something equally stupid and macho when Sheila touched my shoulder at the base of my neck. My tension dissolved. Sheila smiled sweetly at the clerk and asked for some passes for another night. The teenager blushed and mumbled an agreement.

"It's okay," Sheila told me. "We can see it tomorrow. Let's go have some dessert and coffee."

"Uh, okay." Yeah, I was a smooth talker.

I didn't know what she had seen in me that she wanted to help bring out. I had no idea why she could calm me down when no one else could, not even myself. I just knew I was lucky to be with her, and no one should ever get between us.

After a few more clunks, the machine spit out some ice. I was heading back to the room when Wendy popped her head out the door.

"She's waking up!"

I broke into a run, not worrying when some ice cubes bounced out of the bucket and hit the sidewalk. I almost slipped as I skidded into the room.

She's awake! Orson shouted.

I kneeled beside the bed. Sheila was stirring, her eyes cracking open. I rubbed an ice cube on her lips.

"My boys..."

I sighed in relief. "Welcome back. You had us worried."

She hugged me weakly with one arm. "Me too."

Orson tried to jump on the bed, but he didn't quite make it. I caught him in midair and hoisted him up next to Sheila. Orson's tail wagged nonstop, and he bounced all around her. After he almost landed on her head, I grabbed his collar to settle him down. Sheila put her arm around him, and he nuzzled her as he snuggled in close to her.

"Can you talk?" I asked her.

"A little. I'm very tired."

Orson whined and put his paws on her chest. *I missed you.*

"I missed you, too."

Mama, why did you leave?

I was glad Orson asked that question because I was dying to know.

"It's complicated."

I looked down into her eyes. "Sheila, I got that from the coven for weeks. You can tell us."

"I will, but I'm so tired…"

That almost sounded like an excuse, but I wasn't going to push it. We'd all been through a lot that night. "Okay, honey. Get some rest. We'll talk in the morning."

She closed her eyes. After a minute, her breathing evened out, and she started to snore softly. Orson buried his face in her side. After another minute, he was asleep as well. His snores weren't particularly soft, but I knew Sheila wouldn't mind. I stood and walked over to sit in a chair at the rickety table.

"Are you okay?" Wendy asked.

I shrugged. "Yeah, I guess."

"What's wrong?"

"It's just that we've been after her for so long, and now that we got her, I just… I don't know."

"You thought it would be over?"

I nodded. "Yeah."

"But it's not."

"No, it's not. She still won't say why she left. We still have to worry about Yareth. I just want to take her home."

"She'll tell you in the morning. Besides, she *is* home." Wendy pointed at the bed where Sheila and Orson were all nestled together. "Her family's here."

I knew what she meant. But I couldn't stop fearing that things wouldn't be the same.

THIRTY-FIVE

WENDY AND I DECIDED WE should take turns being a lookout. Whether it was through magic or homing devices, Yareth always seemed to be one step ahead of us. Hopefully, he would be too busy tending to his wounds and playing with the stone to bother us for a while. Wendy took the first shift. I lay for an hour, but sleep never came. Eventually, I got up and told Wendy to get some rest.

I sat by the window while Wendy curled up on the second bed. Sheila and Orson hadn't moved. The lights were off, and I peered through a crack in the curtain, making sure no one came down the road.

Orson's words kept going through my head. *Mama, why did you leave?*

I really wanted to know the answer to that question. Even if she was worried about Yareth going after Orson and me, she had to know that we would do everything we could to find her. It had been so long since I felt I could trust someone, and I would have put my life in Sheila's hands. So I didn't understand why she hadn't trusted me.

The sky slowly brightened to gray then pink as the sun started to rise. Soon Sheila would be awake, and we'd get some answers.

I got up and went over to the bed. I gently shook Wendy's shoulder. She opened her eyes and bolted upright.

I patted her arm. "Everything's okay. I'm going to find us some breakfast. If anything happens, call me on this."

I held up the second of the Walmart disposable phones. Surprisingly, the fleabag motel had notepads by the phone. I scratched out my number and gave it to Wendy, then I headed for the door.

At a roadside greasy spoon a few miles down the road, I bought three egg sandwiches, three coffees, and an order of sausage patties. Juggling the sack and cups, I hurried back out to the car. On the return trip to the motel, I checked for suspicious vehicles but saw nothing out of the ordinary.

Back in the room, nothing had changed. I started unpacking the sack of food on the small table. Even though the diner had been open less than half an hour, the coffee already smelled burnt and stale.

I chuckled as I handed a cup to Wendy. "The coffee is definitely not a small batch Cuban roast. A small Cuban man made it, though."

Wendy gave me a tired smile. "As long as it has caffeine."

"It's not decaf, so that's something."

I looked over at Sheila and Orson. Sheila's hand rested on Orson's head, and he drooled happily on her arm. "They're so happy. Like none of this ever happened."

Wendy nodded. "There's no bond quite like that between a witch and her familiar."

"Do you have one?"

"I did. A cat. Minnaloushe."

"Minnow what?"

"Min-ah-loush. I read it in a poem in college. Yeats. It was about a black cat, and the name sounded pretty. And she was a beautiful cat, black as coal with eyes like diamonds."

"What happened to her?"

"She died. She was eighteen, and her kidneys were failing." Her eyes glistened with tears. "That was ten years ago. I can still feel her, and I can still feel how much of a hole she left in me."

"You've never gotten another one?"

She shook her head. "I couldn't take that loss again. It's rare for a witch to get another familiar after having been so close to one."

I pulled out two of the sandwiches and passed her one. "Huh. Sheila did."

Wendy gave me a puzzled look. "What do you mean?"

"She had a cat when she was young. Orson came along when that cat was old and sick."

She paused with her sandwich halfway to her mouth. "That's... that never happens. You don't find a familiar until you're active as a witch. Things happen that you can't really explain. Like you think about ice cream, and the ice cream truck drives by. Or you wish you could have a necklace, and it magically turns up in your pocket. Then you learn about magic, then you sometimes find a familiar who can act as a guide."

"Sheila said she was eight when the cat came. She said she could hear her mother thinking."

From Wendy's shocked expression, I might as well have told her that I rode there on a unicorn. *"What?"*

I put my sandwich down in the pool of congealed bacon grease on the wax wrapper. "Um, that's not normal? I mean, I know it's not normal... but, you know, normal for witches."

"No. It is not. It's rare for anyone to have ability before puberty. The mind is simply not formed yet. But she..." She stared at Sheila and Orson on the bed.

"What?"

"Do you understand how strong she must be?"

"Honestly, no. She doesn't talk to me about it all that much."

"And to find a second familiar right away... and to be able to talk to him..."

"Come on. You can talk to Orson. Heck, *I* can talk to Orson, and I can't even do card tricks."

"Until two days ago, I would have told you that I might be the strongest witch in Florida. Yes, I can talk to Orson. Very well. In fact, I talk to him easier than I could talk to Minnaloushe."

"What do you mean?"

"Most animals can't talk."

"No kidding."

Wendy glared at me. "I'm serious. Familiars are very friendly, but most of them can't handle concepts like human speech and thought patterns. Like most pets, they can recognize words that you say often. But to have a conversation, that's really special. And to converse with someone non-magical? That's just unheard of." She shook her head. "And she never told you how rare that was?"

I shrugged. "I really have no point of comparison. I never knew a real witch before, and the ones in Sheila's coven don't care much for me. None of them have a familiar that I'm aware of. Do you think that's why Yareth is so intent on getting his hands on Orson?"

"It could be."

"You didn't seem too fazed by Orson when we met. I mean, you never mentioned that he was special or that it was odd you could talk to him."

"I was curious. I wanted to see how strong he was. And he's incredible. If he picked Sheila, that means she's incredible too."

I looked over at the bed. Sheila's hair was draped over the pillow, and her forehead glowed with sweat. She was still radiant. "I know."

I pulled a Styrofoam clamshell out of the bag and opened it. Orson stirred almost immediately, which I had figured would happen. He would never sleep through the smell of sausage wafting across the room. He stretched and yawned before jumping off the bed. The squeaky springs in the cheap mattress woke Sheila.

I smiled at her. "Welcome back, babe."

"Gabriel—" She coughed.

I grabbed the cup of water from the nightstand and held it to her mouth. She drank a little then lay back on the pillow.

"I have some coffee and a sandwich for you if you can manage them."

"In a minute."

You didn't forget me, did you? Orson asked.

"You have to ask?" I put the container with the sausage patties down on the floor in front of him.

Sheila sat up. "What is that?"

"Orson's breakfast."

She put a hand to her chest as if I had just served him some week-old roadkill. "What have you been feeding him?"

"Food. He loves it."

Yeah, I love it.

"He can't eat that stuff!"

Sure I can.

"Where's his kibble?"

I shook my head. "Honey, we've been looking for you for weeks. I didn't think to stop at Petco on the way here."

She pursed her lips as she stared down at Orson, who was scarfing up the sausage as if afraid she would take it away. "All right. But we are finding him better food the minute we get out of here." She eyed me steadily. "And I suppose you haven't been eating any better?"

I was relieved. She was the same old Sheila, more concerned about our diet than the fact that a magician had tried to exile her soul from her body. "Do I have to eat kibble too?"

Sheila laughed. It was dry and raspy, but it was a beautiful sound. "Maybe. How many hamburgers have you eaten?"

"Big Macs aren't hamburgers. The FDA said so."

We both grinned. I enjoyed bantering with her, but we were dancing around the questions.

I tried a more direct approach. "Sheila, why did you go?"

The smile left her face, and she closed her eyes. "It's complicated."

"We've got time."

She sighed. "All right."

She coughed softly, and I gave her some more water. I then handed her a cup of coffee, though it had become lukewarm. Maybe that would improve the taste.

She took another sip of water. "Last month, Ramona sent me out to find something in Florida. She had heard about an object of great power, something very magical."

I held up a finger. "Let me guess. A big purple crystal about as big as a toy football? And it boosts your power considerably."

"Yes, I see you might be familiar with it. She has her sources. Ramona's always been worried about the coven, and she sometimes gets a little paranoid."

I rolled my eyes. "Yeah, a little."

Sheila frowned. "Stop that! She has reason to be. You haven't known her that long. She could tell you stories about the things she's had to deal with. She and her mom got run out of their hometown when she was a teenager, and all because she overheard some thoughts she wasn't supposed to. It was a Bible Belt town, and she heard the preacher think some decidedly un-Christian thoughts about some of the younger girls in the congregation. He found out and whipped the town into a frenzy by calling her a demon. She swears there were people carrying torches, and they barely got out with their lives. Ever since then, she's been obsessed with keeping her coven safe. When she learned about a powerful gem that could amplify her abilities, she knew she had to have it. She figured the coven would be protected from anything if she could use that."

Sheila paused to drink some more water. "Anyway, I went down to St. Augustine and poked around, but I couldn't find anything. That happens sometimes. Ramona hears whispers, but they aren't always right."

"But not this time."

Sheila coughed. "No. Someone had beaten us to it."

"Yareth."

"No, not Yareth."

"What? You mean someone else got there?"

"No, his name is David."

"Oh. Well, I didn't think Yareth was his real name."

"No, you don't understand. *David*."

I was confused. I looked over at Wendy. She just shrugged.

Sheila cleared her throat. "I'm talking about David, Lisa's ex. Yareth *is* Lisa's ex."

My mouth fell open. That certainly cleared up a few things, like why he was so fixated on Orson and why Lisa's cousin Madison was in the middle of everything. The craziness was more than a rivalry between magic users. It was personal.

Once I got over the surprise, I said, "You never told me David knew magic."

"I didn't think he did. I didn't know until a few weeks ago. Lisa never said a word about it. Maybe he made her teach him something, and she was too embarrassed to tell me. That would have been just like him. 'Prove you love me. Teach me some tricks.'" Sheila scowled. "But Lisa wouldn't have taught him anything powerful."

"Okay. So what happened next?"

"Well, after that first trip, I came back home to tell Ramona I couldn't find the artifact. The funny thing was, before I even came in the door, I could tell she already knew it."

"Because Yareth—I mean, David had called her."

She nodded. "Right."

"And said he had something she wanted."

"Yes."

"And maybe he'd trade for it."

"What do you need me for? I should go back to sleep." She and settled her head on the thin pillow.

Orson barked his displeasure.

She rubbed his scruff. "Don't worry. I'm still here."

"So what did he want? Orson?"

"Yes."

Wendy shook her head. "That makes absolutely no sense. If he has any idea what he's doing, he'd know you can't just trade familiars like Pokémon cards."

I gaped at her.

Wendy shrugged. "I have a nephew."

Sheila sat up and took a sip of coffee. From the way she grimaced, the brew's flavor hadn't improved with a change in temperature. "Wendy, you know Orson can talk to you, and he can talk to Gabe. He's very strong. David must have found out about him through Lisa and figured that if Orson makes me stronger, then Orson would make *him* stronger. And Orson and that rock combined would make him even stronger than that."

I was still confused. "But why? To what end?"

Sheila sighed. "David was always a nasty piece of work. He could be charming when it suited him, but he never was to me. Or to Lisa that I ever noticed. He blamed me for breaking them up. He said I poisoned her with all this witch nonsense."

"So he thinks he can become a super-warlock, and then he can... what? Cast a spell on Lisa? Make her love him?"

"Something like that."

I wanted to scream. Sheila had been missing for weeks, people had tried to kill me, and Orson had been dognapped, all because some asshole couldn't get over a breakup. *Go watch* The Notebook *and eat some ice cream and leave us out of it.* But that still left a little gap in the story.

Orson asked before I could. *Mama, why did you leave?*

I nodded. "Yeah. We could have helped you fight Yareth or David or whoever."

Sheila's eyes teared up. "It wasn't that simple."

The pack stays together. I couldn't tell if Orson was angry or sad. I couldn't tell what I was, either.

She patted Orson's head. "I had to go. I had to keep you safe."

That didn't cut it for me. "I can handle that asshole. I can handle him a lot better now that I know you're all right."

"No! That's not it. I had to come back down here because Ramona made me. She took the deal. She told me to give Orson to David and get the stone."

"What?" I recoiled. "You told her who you were dealing with, right? You told her it was Lisa's abusive ex, didn't you?"

"I did. She said that stone was too powerful to be left in some idiot's hands. She thought the gem would strengthen the coven. As far as she was concerned, if that meant trading some dog for the stone, then so be it."

Wendy gasped. "I have never... I've never heard of any priestess doing that. Ordering a follower to do that, to give up her familiar, it's... that's just..."

It's bullshit.

Sheila rubbed Orson's neck. "Yes, I had the same feeling."

Orson drooled happily. *You'd never give me away, would you?*

She hugged him close. "Never! Even when you left a dead rat in my slipper."

You didn't like my present? He whined and gave her sad eyes.

"I'm more of a Tiffany's girl." She winked at me. "I could

never give Orson away. But the coven has helped me out with so much. I hoped I might be able to get the stone a different way."

I still wasn't happy with the explanation. "There are limits! You could have said no. You could have told me. We could have helped you with Ramona."

Her shoulders slumped. "You don't understand. When I came to New York, I didn't know anyone. I found Lisa's shop almost by accident, and she recognized what I was. She took me in, and she introduced me to Ramona. If it weren't for her and Lisa, I don't know where I would have wound up or if I'd even still be alive. Ramona found me my apartment. In fact, she owns the building. She's not just my friend and mentor; she's my landlord. She's never charged me rent. She just asks me to do those errands for the coven."

"You mean you were doing what she said to because you got a sweet deal on rent?" My blood pressure rose. Even though I was trying to fight it, I could hear my voice getting louder. "Come on! We could have found a place without her."

"It's not about money! How could you think that?"

"Then what was it about?"

"She said she would hurt you!"

Wendy gasped. I opened and closed my mouth a couple of times.

Sheila coughed and sipped some water. "She said to take Orson down there and get the stone. If I didn't, she said she could make it so I wouldn't see you again."

My anger returned like a bad old friend. "Does that skinny bitch think she could hurt me?" I really wanted Ramona to walk through that door and try.

"Yes. And she could! She'd never fight you directly, but she could make you forget things. Like where you live. Like looking both ways before crossing the street. There are any number of things she could make you do without you even realizing it."

I recalled that time when I had tried to go to that coven meeting and somehow couldn't find the door. It wouldn't have taken much for Ramona to distract me enough for me to fall in an open manhole or something like that. I unclenched my fists. Little white half-circles were in my palms where I had dug my fingernails in them. I took Sheila's hand. "I'm sorry. I'm so sorry. I had no idea. That must have been awful for you."

She brushed my cheek with her fingertips. "I was never going to give up Orson, but I couldn't let her do anything to you, either. I had to see what David wanted and if he would give up the stone or if I could somehow take it from him. So I told her I would go as long as she promised to leave you alone. And I wasn't about to take Orson with me in case David tried to snatch him." She shook her head. "That didn't go so well."

"Yeah, I met one of David's little helpers. He said you were pretty pissed."

Sheila blushed. She was embarrassed that she'd gotten mad, even though her anger was completely justified. It was adorable. "Sorry," she mumbled.

"Don't feel bad. We've done lots worse to little Morty since then."

She didn't ask what I meant. She likely, rightfully, didn't want to know. "After that, I was kind of stuck. I didn't want to go back home because I was afraid of what Ramona might do to you. I didn't want to call you because I didn't want you to bring Orson down and risk David getting him. And I was afraid of Ramona catching on to what was happening. The safest place was going into the trance. Ramona had promised not to hurt you as long as I was in Florida. And David couldn't get Orson as long as I was in the trance. I haven't had to go there in a long time, not since I was young and things were bad at home. It was relaxing and peaceful, and back then, no amount of my mom and my stepfather's screaming would disturb me." She paused to wipe her eyes. "I'm sorry I made you worry, but I couldn't think of anything else to do. It seemed like the best thing to do at the time."

"I had Orson in New York. Why didn't Ramona just take him then?"

"She couldn't. Not if she wanted Orson to cooperate and not if she wanted him to be able to help. Like Wendy said, you can't just trade familiars like cards. There's a ceremony."

I snorted. "There's always a ceremony."

Sheila ignored my sarcasm. "A witch can release her familiar. But she would have to do it willingly. And I never would. And they couldn't threaten me if I was in the trance."

"Why did you pick that place?" I asked. "That abandoned resort was terrible."

She frowned. "It seemed secluded. It was all boarded up, and I figured no one would find me there. I couldn't stay at a hotel. Some maid might have freaked out and called 9-1-1 if she found me like that. And I know you have friends who can track credit cards. You would have found me right away. Plus, I can only come out of the trance when I want to; no one can make me."

"Except you couldn't last night."

"Yes. David must have found a way to keep me trapped. That stone is extremely powerful if a novice like him can use it that easily."

Something didn't make sense. "You said Lisa never mentioned David being magic, right?"

"Right. Maybe he learned something from her, but she never told me. And she would have never taught him anything destructive."

"And she kicked him out about a year ago, right?"

"Yes."

"That's about when he showed up down here," Wendy added.

"And he was already talking big about how he was Mr. Magic Man then?"

Wendy nodded. "That's right."

"So when did he learn destructive magic like that? And how? You don't get it by having it rub off on you. I should know."

Sheila blushed a bright red.

I realized what I said. "Oh! I'm sorry! I didn't mean... I, uh..."

Wendy busted out laughing. Orson howled in delight. Soon, we were all laughing. It felt good. For the first time in a month, I could relax completely and enjoy myself.

But I couldn't get the questions out of my head. *How did he learn that much magic? Was the stone that powerful, or was there something else going on?*

THIRTY-SIX

W E STAYED IN THE HOTEL that day. Sheila was still weak from the trance. She sent me out for food and dog kibble. I suspected she wanted to talk shop with Wendy, but I didn't push it. I could tell Orson wasn't pleased about returning to a kibble diet, but he was so happy to have his mama back that he kept quiet about it.

"Don't worry about a thing," Wendy said when she came over to close the door behind me. "I'll take care of her. I've been shielding us since we got here. There's no way anyone will find us."

It was nice to get out of the room for a bit. It was a beautiful day, sunny enough to keep the top down but not so hot that I would melt in a puddle of sweat. I thought about Sheila sitting in that abandoned resort room with no air conditioning for two weeks and shivered. I didn't know how that trance worked, and I was amazed she had made it out alive. I got thirsty just from walking two blocks in the sun.

On the drive back from the store, I wondered what we should do next. I wanted to leave, but we couldn't go home. Sheila couldn't trust her coven, and I would be in danger. And maybe Ramona would just take Orson after all. And if we left that stone in Florida, that would leave Wendy to deal with a pissed-off magician and his cronies.

I thought about angry, matricidal Madison, who was willing to bug her cousin's phone for the jealous ex then introduce him to a group of witches. She had also found him a place to work out of by playing on another person's affections. I really hoped there weren't a whole lot more disciples like her.

When I got back to the motel, I paid the clerk for another day. He never looked up when I put my money down. Walking down the sidewalk to the room, I heard shouts and barks. I sprinted the remaining distance. I dropped the groceries and banged on the door.

Wendy opened it then went back to yelling at Sheila before I had even stepped inside. "You're crazy! Matthew totally lucked out in marrying Lady Mary!"

Sheila held up her hand. "No way! Mary was lucky anyone would have her after that Turkish affair!"

I don't know who those people are! Orson whined.

I looked between them. "Hey, keep it down! David can probably hear you in Orlando."

"Sorry," Wendy said. "We get about five channels in here, and PBS had a *Downton Abbey* marathon. It's so nice to get a chance to talk about it with someone. Most of my regulars only want to argue about the Seminoles or the Gators."

Sheila stared at her blankly.

"College football," I explained.

Sheila smiled. "Oh good. Nothing important."

Wendy and I laughed. After I gathered up what groceries hadn't been left splattered outside, we unpacked the food and spread it on the table. I put some kibble on a paper plate for Orson.

He whined pitifully. *Really? I thought we were friends.*

I pointed at the unappetizing brown nuggets. "It's good for you. Organic."

Cyanide is organic.

Sheila waggled a finger at Orson. "Now stop. You've been eating terribly, and you need better nutrition. Eat it."

Orson bowed his head in defeat and started munching on his kibble. He would never disobey Sheila.

I peeled an orange in solidarity. "It seems to me that we still haven't fixed anything."

Sheila nodded. "You're right. David still has the stone. He still wants Orson, and Ramona wants me to trade him."

"And I can't go back to my shop while he's out there," Wendy added. "If he still has the stone, I can't take the chance he won't try to wreck the place again."

Sheila put down her sandwich. "And we can't go back home. If I go back without the stone, then Ramona might do something to Gabriel."

"Do you think Ramona told the others about her plan?" I asked. "And if so, would the rest of them support her?"

"I wouldn't think so. But then, I never would have believed Ramona would be this way. Lisa would never be on board with it. I'm sure of that. There's no way she'd help out David. Ramona must not have told her."

"So you're certain Lisa isn't in on this?"

"No. Absolutely not. After everything she told me about him, I can't imagine her doing more than spitting on him if she passed him on the street."

I nodded. "I talked to Lisa a few times. She was always helpful. She seemed genuinely concerned for you, but I was afraid she might have been tipping off David."

"Why would you think that?"

"Because I would talk to her, and then David would pop up where I said I was going to be. But now I think her phone was bugged, probably by Madison."

Sheila slapped the table. "That little bitch! Lisa had a restraining order against David. Madison was the only other person there when we moved Lisa into her new place. David must have gotten to Madison and charmed her into helping him. She was always jealous of Lisa. She wanted to learn magic. Lisa was willing to teach her, but she wasn't going fast enough for Madison's taste."

"Okay. So Madison and David and maybe ten other people control this stone. We can't leave it with them. We saw what they did to Wendy's shop. If we hadn't come by when we did, the whole place would be trashed. We can't let them loose on Florida with that kind of power. We can't go home without it. And we are not trading Orson for it."

The women nodded.

"That leaves us one choice. Get the stone, and shut that asshole down."

Okay. How do we do that?

Sheila picked up her sandwich again. "Yeah, Gabriel, how do we do that?"

"I've got an idea."

THIRTY-SEVEN

L ISA PICKED UP ON THE second ring. I sat next to Sheila so I could listen in on the call. Orson lay next to her with his head on her lap. It would take some time before he was willing to be very far away from her.

Sheila said, "It's me."

"Sheila! Oh, thank Goddess. You don't know how worried I was."

"Listen, I can't talk long, but I have to ask you something." She scratched behind his ear.

"Of course. I'm so happy you're all right."

"Lisa, it's okay. Everything's going to be fine. Now, I need you to listen. Did Ramona say anything about me, about where I had gone?"

"Not much. She said you had gone down to Florida to find something very important. She said we shouldn't worry, even if you were gone a while. Oh, and she told us not to tell anyone. She pointed at me when she said *anyone*." Lisa sniffled. "Sheila, I'm sorry, but I told Gabriel. I know that's who Ramona was talking about, but he was so worried about you." Lisa sounded so sad that she'd disobeyed the coven.

Sheila wagged her finger at me in mock anger then laughed. "That's okay. I'm glad you did. Now, I need you to do something to help me out, okay?"

"Sure. Anything."

"Tell Ramona that everything's almost done, but there's

been a snag in the negotiations. I need her to come down to Orlando to smooth things over."

"Negotiations? What are you—"

"Just make sure you tell her that exactly. She needs to be here tomorrow night at six."

"Where?"

Sheila frowned at me. I stifled a laugh. Before the call, I had come up with the perfect place for a rendezvous. It was very public. I had no desire to get ambushed, and I figured a crowd would keep everyone's worst impulses in check. It also had the additional benefit of annoying Ramona. I waved my hand at the phone.

Sheila gave a barely audible sigh and rolled her eyes. She was used to my sense of humor, but that didn't mean she liked it. "The Holy Land Experience."

"Really? Are you sure?" Lisa asked.

"It's the last place Yareth would look for us. She needs to be there at six o'clock tomorrow evening. We'll be in the Garden of Gethsemane."

"I guess. It's just that it's not really your kind of place."

"Don't worry about it. Just tell Ramona exactly what I said. Got it?"

"Okay, Sheila. Stay safe, and come home soon."

Sheila hung up then punched my arm. "You just couldn't resist, could you?"

"Come on. You have to admit that it's the last place Ramona or Yareth would think of."

"It's just so tacky!"

"Says the girl who can't get enough of *Bewitched*."

She threw a pillow at me. "What? Eudora's my role model."

The Holy Land Experience was an interactive theme park where religious tourists could watch their Lord and Savior be crucified five times a day. It was kind of like the

Hall of Presidents at Disney but with significantly more scourging. It wasn't my idea of a great afternoon, but different strokes and all that.

Sheila sat next to me on a bench in the Garden of Gethsemane. "Are you sure about this?" Orson lay at her feet. Wendy was stationed across the plaza so she could watch the perimeter. The garden was a quiet spot and actually quite pretty.

I grinned. "I'm sure we can get a pretty good spot to watch the Crucifixion Parade if we hurry."

She slapped my arm. "Stop it. I hate when you joke like that. It's called the Passion. It's a free country, remember?"

"I'm sorry. I'm nervous, and this is how I deal with it."

"I know. Do you think this plan is going to work?"

I shrugged. "Well, we know Madison bugged Lisa's phone, so it's a good bet David heard your call. And if Lisa did what you asked, Ramona will come to claim her stone. With any luck, they'll both show up, and we can sort this out."

Sheila let out a single low laugh. "How do you figure?"

"Maybe I can convince them through eloquent words that you have no intention of trading Orson for a rock."

Or I can bite them. Like hamburger. Orson was still a little ornery from having to eat dog food again.

I scratched his neck. "Yeah, buddy. There's always that."

Yareth was never going to willingly let go of his special toy. And Ramona wasn't going to tell Sheila "Just kidding!" about the whole give-up-your-dog thing. I just wanted them to leave Sheila alone. And I could be very persuasive when I wanted to be.

I checked my watch. It was a quarter till six. If Ramona or Yareth were coming, they would be there in the next fifteen minutes. I stood. "If Ramona sees me, she'll know something's up. I'm going to hide across the way with Wendy." I reached down for Orson's leash. He hadn't been any happier about wearing a leash than he was about the kibble, but the park rules demanded it.

Sheila put her foot on the end of the leash. "If Orson's not here, then Ramona will suspect something. She must know you came down here."

I kissed her and held her close. "I love you."

"I love you, too."

Get a room.

I jogged over to Wendy's hiding place near the entrance to a replica of the Dead Sea Scroll caves. There were metal detectors at the gate, so Wendy had left her shotgun in the car. Apparently, turning the other cheek only went so far. I didn't think rock salt would help much, anyway.

"Is she okay?" Wendy asked.

"She's got a brave face on, but I can tell she's nervous."

"I don't blame her."

It was near the end of the day, so the crowd was thinning out. I would have expected a tall woman dressed in the blue robes Ramona always wore would stand out, but half the employees were dressed in togas.

Then I spotted her striding across the square. I tugged on Wendy's sleeve, and we ducked back behind the cave wall. I needn't have worried. Ramona was focused intently on Sheila and Orson. When she reached the bench, she sat down next to Sheila. I wouldn't be able to hear anything from that distance, so I moved to edge around and find a closer hiding spot.

Wendy grabbed my arm and shook her head. She closed her eyes and bowed her head. A moment later, I could hear their voices as if I were standing right next to them.

"Hello, dear," Ramona said.

"Hello, Priestess."

"You don't have to be so formal."

"I know. This just feels so awkward."

"It's all right. I'm just glad you've come around and decided to do what's right." Ramona beamed. She was completely convinced of her rightness, and how anyone could be against her was a puzzle.

"Don't tell me what's right. How can you ask me to give up Orson?"

Orson whined and rubbed his body against Sheila's leg.

Ramona sighed. "We've been through this. You'll find another familiar. You have before."

Sheila shook her head. "You don't know that."

"You're stronger than most witches. But just think. With that stone, we would never have to worry about interlopers like David again. You and I could set a standard for witchcraft. We could protect all the struggling neophytes. Remember when you came to me, how lost you were? With this much power, we could be a beacon for anyone who needs us. That stone is stronger than anything I've seen."

"Stronger than our faith? Stronger than our bond, Ramona? Than mine and Orson's bond?"

Ramona stared at Sheila as if she were stupid. "Yes. It's stronger than all of that."

Sheila shook her head. "Love is the most powerful magic. That's what we're taught."

"That's nice. You hang on to love when some crazy bunch of fundamentalists tries to burn you at the stake."

"You're the one in the blue robes. I don't think I'll be first one someone comes after."

"I'm serious. You may think it was centuries ago, but burnings still happen. *Beheadings* happen. You can't afford to be naïve."

"When did you get so hard?"

"Not hard. Strong. Sheila, you're sweet. You really are. But I've doing this a long time. I've had to deal with men trying to control me, suppress me, and dominate me my whole life."

"It's not any better when it comes from another woman controlling you."

"Sheila, just listen. I know you think I'm being harsh. I'm not. I'm just being realistic. You of all people should understand."

Sheila stiffened. From all she had told me about her childhood, I knew she did understand. I also knew she was a lot tougher than Ramona gave her credit for. I hoped she could keep from lashing out until Yareth showed up. I knew I wouldn't have been able to.

Ramona ignored Sheila's stricken look and continued. "When I was young, concepts like 'women's lib' barely existed. I grew up a second-class citizen, with men being condescending and patronizing me. When I found my power, it was the happiest day of my life. I vowed that no one would ever take advantage of me or talk down to me again. Ever." She leaned closer to Sheila. "And I will do whatever I think is necessary to make sure that no one can hurt our coven. We will be strong. I've never seen an artifact that powerful. If some idiot like David can use it, then think what we can do."

"You know David is the one who has it? Did you tell Lisa?"

"No. Why make her worry? David is a punk who thinks he's important. Once we get that stone away from him, he'll be nothing again."

I scanned the area for Yareth. I didn't seem him anywhere. I hoped we hadn't been wrong about the bugged phone.

Sheila said, "He'll be a bitter nothing who will have my familiar."

Orson whined and looked up at Ramona with his big, sad eyes.

She ignored him. "I'm sorry, but sacrifices must be made to get that stone."

"What is that thing?" Sheila asked. "I've never seen anything like it."

"As far as I can tell, it seems to be a crystal from Eastern

206

Europe. It was smuggled out by a gypsy witch fleeing persecution. She probably ran to the new world, thinking it would protect her. She must have gotten to Florida and hid it before she died. If I had to guess, I'd say that was the reason the Fountain of Youth has its reputation. There was magic there, just not the kind everyone thinks."

With a squawk, the public address system came to life. "Ladies and gentlemen, the time is now six o'clock. The Holy Land is closing for the day. Please join the exodus, and return to us tomorrow at ten a.m."

Yareth still hadn't appeared. I was getting seriously worried.

Sheila said, "I still don't like it. There's no reason he should give us the stone. I don't trust him."

"I don't, either. If he doesn't give it up voluntarily, we have other ways."

"You know what he did to Lisa."

"I do. It sickens me."

"Then why? Why are we dealing with him at all, stone or not?" Sheila was doing her best to try to persuade Ramona. I could tell it was killing her to go against her mentor, but I also didn't think it would work. If Ramona was willing to sell out Lisa, she wasn't going to care about a dog or be willing to listen to reason.

Ramona rubbed the bridge of her nose. "Because every second he has that rock is a second that we are vulnerable. If he's dumb enough to trade it for a dog, then all the better for us. That's the last I have to say about it."

Orson whimpered. I wished I could pet him. *Hold on, boy. It's all right.*

A security guard strolled up to the bench. "Excuse me, ladies. The park is closing. You're going to have to go."

Ramona looked up at him. "Oh, that's okay. You saw us leave. We aren't here. You can go home now."

His eyes went glassy for a second, then he nodded. "That's right. You did leave already. I must be getting tired.

Time to head home!" He turned and ambled off toward the park entrance.

A few stragglers passed, but they didn't pay any attention to us. I didn't spot Yareth or any of his minions.

Ramona put a hand on Sheila's arm. "I am not asking. I am sorry you'll have to give up the dog. I am. But this is just too important. I can't allow that bastard to have that much power."

"Oh, you can't? I beg to differ."

I jumped a little, wondering how David had gotten so close without my seeing him. He only had two of his acolytes with him, Madison and Morty. David was in the middle, holding the stone. The two Ms were on either side of him, each with one hand resting on the rock. But the oddest thing was that all three were floating several inches above the ground. I realized that they had floated over the outside wall. I guessed badasses like them thought they didn't have to pay for tickets. They touched down and strode toward the bench.

A new guard turned the corner and entered the plaza. "Excuse me! The park is closed! You'll have to leave."

Madison gave a violent sweep of her arm, and the guard was flung aside like a rag doll. He crashed into a palm tree and crumpled to the ground. He didn't get up. I hoped he was okay, but I couldn't leave our hiding spot to check.

David faced Ramona and Sheila. "Now, I believe it's time to get my dog."

Ramona stood up and stared him down. "There's no need for cheap theatrics. We are all here. We've all agreed to do the exchange. Now calm down and give me the stone."

David chuckled. He sounded like an ass when he did that. "Oh, you must think me a stupid child. The dog first, and then the stone."

Orson growled.

Ramona shook her head. "You know the dog is no good to you unless Sheila releases it."

"Well, then make her release it."

"Not until we get the stone."

David passed the stone to Madison and gestured at her and Morty. "Go on."

Madison strode toward the bench. Morty hesitated, obviously having second thoughts about the whole Dark Lord thing. Rock salt and alligators could have that effect on a person. After another wave of David's hand, Morty limped after her. David then stood alone with his back to me. If it came to it, I could probably jump him before he could do anything.

Ramona nudged Sheila. "Go to her."

Sheila inched forward slowly, almost dragging a reluctant Orson. All parties met in the middle. A nervous Morty held out his hand for Orson's leash.

David shouted, "Enough stalling! The dog!"

Sheila said, "Until I release him, Orson's not going to go with you." She knelt down next to Orson. "It's okay. They can't hurt you." He didn't look as though he believed her. She hugged him and made him face her. "Trust me. It will be fine."

Orson didn't look happy, but he bobbed his head. Sheila passed the leash over to Morty. Orson growled, and Morty looked as if he were going to pee his pants. If Madison hadn't glared at him, he probably would have run away.

Sheila said, "Orson, play nice."

Orson whined and pouted. Morty tugged, but Orson stayed locked in place. When Orson didn't want to move, he wasn't moving. Many times, I'd tried to get him outside when it was too cold or rainy for his tastes. He wasn't a heavy dog, but if he planted his feet, that was it. I didn't know if it was magic or good old-fashioned stubbornness. Morty took two steps and almost fell over when Orson pulled back on the leash. Morty tried to drag him, but Orson just glared and growled.

"Come on, you stupid mutt," Morty said.

I smirked. That had never worked for me, either.

Ramona shook her head. "He's not going with you until I get the stone."

Sheila bristled. "Yes, Ramona. *I* will tell Orson to move once *I* get the stone."

I whispered to Wendy, "If by some chance Madison actually hands over the rock, we need to focus on getting Orson back. Ramona can have that stupid stone for all I care, and Sheila can keep her from interfering."

Wendy shook her head. "That's not going to happen. I'm sure he told Madison to hang on to it."

"Of course. But he'll also be a pompous ass and make some pronouncement about it. In that case, we rush him mid-diatribe and take him down. Sound good?"

"I'll leave the heavy stuff to you. I've got some spells I haven't had a chance to try out yet. I can't *wait* for a little practice." She flexed her fingers and gave me a wicked grin.

Ramona called out, "The stone, David. Now."

He scowled. "That is no longer my name!"

Sheila smirked. "Sure. *Yareth.* Whatever. You can use any name you like, but I still know what you are."

David glared at her. "Oh really? And what is that?"

"You're a cheap little bully. Now you think you know magic, but you think it's just about having a way to push people around. It is so much more than that."

His eyes popped wide, and his nostrils flared. Sheila had hit a nerve. I didn't know if that was a good thing, but at least he'd be distracted. I got ready to jump.

"You know nothing about me!" David screamed. "You bitches were always jealous of anyone who had real power!"

"You have two things wrong. First, that's 'witches.'" Ramona waved her hand, and the stone floated up out of Madison's hands. "And second, you have no power over us."

That caught David short, but he recovered. He lunged

forward and grabbed onto the stone. Madison reached up for it as well. Morty was still struggling with Orson, but he stopped for a second to gape at the battle for the rock.

Wendy jumped to her feet. "That's our cue!"

We ran for the plaza.

THIRTY-EIGHT

ORTY SPOTTED ME HEADING FOR David and shouted a warning. Fortunately, David and Madison were both occupied with keeping the stone away from Ramona. Ramona was stronger that I would have expected. She didn't even seem to be exerting herself while the wonder twins could barely hang on.

Orson tried to help by barking and nipping at Morty's legs. Morty leapt and spun to avoid the snapping jaws, but he was having a hard time since he wouldn't let go of the leash.

David suddenly stopped struggling to hang onto the rock and let out a loud laugh. "You want it that badly? Then here!"

Madison nodded at David, then they both let go of the rock. David must have given it a little boost because it shot like a rocket straight toward Ramona's head. The big stone clocked her on the jaw, and she crumpled to the ground into a heap. Madison scrambled after the gem, which had landed a few feet away from Ramona. Sheila dodged to the left to intercept her.

David spun around and sneered at me. "I've had enough of you."

"That makes two of us." I swung my right fist, aiming at his face.

He blocked my punch by catching my fist in his hand. I wasn't Bruce Lee, but I could pack a pretty good punch, especially when I was pissed off. So I was stunned by how effortlessly he stopped it.

"You're not in a bar fight. You're dealing with powers you can't imagine." He flexed his hand slightly.

My knees started to buckle. He wasn't overpowering me. My hand didn't hurt. I just somehow felt like crumpling to the ground. My left hand didn't seem to want to move at all. I struggled to stay on my feet.

He leaned over me. "You know what the worst thing is about Florida? The damned insects. Always buzzing. Always nipping at you. I hate them. Still, it's fun when you get to swat a particularly annoying bug. Sometimes, I even like to tear off their wings."

My knees gave up, and I fell to the ground. David grinned maliciously as he let go of my fist and raised his hand over my head. Then a metal trash can flew into his back. He stumbled over me and landed flat on his face on the ground beside me.

Wendy was standing a few feet away. "No rock salt this time, David."

David scrambled to his feet. I got up a little more slowly, but at least my hand was moving again. I looked around to assess the situation. The rock was still lying a few feet from Ramona, who hadn't moved. Madison was throwing things at Sheila—rocks, signs, litter—using her hands and her magic. Sheila was parrying everything easily using some kind of shield spell. With all the magic being tossed around, I wondered if that rock was boosting everyone in the area. Morty was still busy fending off Orson.

Wendy advanced on David. "You have caused me enough problems. You had best leave the state and pay for my repairs."

"Or what? You are in no position to bargain."

"Really?" Wendy raised her arm and snapped her fingers. "Unlike you, I do not enjoy hurting people. But you have done more than enough damage."

David cried out and grabbed his wrist. At the sound, Madison spun around. She waved her hand, and a park bench flew across the plaza.

I yelled to warn Wendy. She got her hands up and managed to turn the bench, but the edge of it caught her square in the chest. She fell backward, flailing her arms.

I jumped at David, hoping to get him before he recovered from whatever she'd done to his arm. I got two steps before some force slammed into me, and I was down again. Lying there, I struggled to breathe. I tried to sit up and realized I couldn't move at all.

David stepped over to stand next to me. "Stop! One move and I will kill him."

Everything had gone to hell. Nothing about our plan had come to pass the way we had hoped. Ramona was either unconscious or dead. Wendy, moaning a few feet from me, wasn't doing a lot better. Morty still clung to Orson's leash, and Madison ran over to scoop up the rock before hustling back to David's side.

I fought my invisible bonds, but whatever spell David had cast on me kept me pinned. I had been stupid to underestimate him. Madison kicked at my head. Fortunately, she was wearing moccasins, so the impact only felt like a small explosion. Orson howled and tried to run toward me, but Morty held the leash, and he seemed rooted in place.

Sheila raised her hands in a casting position. "Let him go."

David smirked. "I don't think so."

Sheila's eyes flared, and a palm tree behind David burst into flames.

David waved his hand, and the weight on my chest doubled. What little air I'd had in my lungs whooshed out. "There are two of us. Even if you do hit one of us, the other will kill him before you can do anything about it."

I tried to inhale, but my lungs wouldn't inflate. I was getting tunnel vision. I could feel the capillaries in my face bursting. I opened and closed my mouth, but that didn't help at all. I thought I heard a crack. I had watched enough autopsies on *Law & Order* to know that it was probably the hyoid bone. That was the number one clue to a cause of death by strangling. What would Jerry Orbach say when he found my body? They put the squeeze on him? No.

"Stop! Stop it! I'll do it! Just let him go!"

I tried to call out, "Sheila, no. Don't," but no sound came from my lips.

"I'll release him," Sheila cried. "I'll release Orson. He'll be yours."

Mama, no!

I tried to shake my head, but that proved impossible.

David glared at her. "No tricks."

"Just let him go," Sheila pleaded.

"Not until it's done."

"You'll kill him!"

David looked down and seemed mildly surprised. I guessed that my face was probably the same shade of purple as that rock by then. He shrugged. "Then you'd better hurry."

Orson stared at Sheila, eyes full of fear and sadness.

Sheila looked back at him. "I'm sorry."

Mama...

"We tried."

No.

Sheila closed her eyes and murmured something. "Mother Goddess, hear my voice and prayer. Your servant for me is no longer needed." She opened her eyes and stared into Orson's. "I release thee."

No, Mama! Don't—

And I couldn't hear him anymore. He was barking like mad, but I couldn't *hear* him.

I wasn't in his pack anymore. He wasn't ours. He was gone.

THIRTY-NINE

SHEILA SLUMPED TO THE GROUND and buried her face in her hands. Morty dragged Orson over to David, who eagerly took the leash and looped the end over his wrist, the one Wendy hadn't damaged.

"Now nothing can stop me!" Almost as an afterthought, David snapped his fingers.

I gasped and sucked down the air.

Madison smiled. "That's right! We'll show them!" She gazed at David adoringly.

The oxygen was returning to my brain slowly, but I could hear something in Madison's voice, an edge of desire and need. She wanted something more from David than just being a cult leader. Maybe I could use that.

"That's right, David!" I wheezed. "Lisa will have no choice but to come crawling back, right?"

Madison froze. "What?"

"Come on, Maddie," I said. "You knew all about Lisa. That's why you bugged her phone."

She frowned. "That was only to keep tabs on her and that useless coven."

"Sure. Keep telling yourself that. David only cared about you if it got him close to Lisa."

David screamed, "Enough!"

The weight slammed back onto my chest, and talking became a problem.

Madison spun to face David. "Is that true?"

David shook his head. "I never used you. I helped you develop your potential. But you've never been more than an adept to me. Lisa has always been my true love, and she won't get away from me now."

Madison scowled. Her eyes got dangerous. "That's what this was about? Getting your stupid cow girlfriend back?"

"*Do not* talk about her like that!"

"She did nothing but hold me back and keep you down. And you want to go back to that? Are you crazy?"

"Madison, do not say or do anything you'll regret." He flexed his hands theatrically.

His attention was all on her, and the weight lifted off me a bit. I was able to pull in a shallow breath.

"Have you not seen what we've done together?" Madison cried. "Don't you understand why I helped you? I killed my mother for you!"

"You have been very helpful, but you're not the one in charge here. Do not forget that."

"Oh, I'm not?" Madison raised the stone. "Then why don't you stop me?" She swung the stone at his head.

David tried to raise his hands, either to block the blow or cast a spell, but it didn't matter. He was too slow. The rock slammed into his face. There was a loud crack, and he dropped to the ground.

Madison swung again and again. "You thought you were running things? That's what I *let* you think!"

David's face was a bloody pulp. His nose didn't even protrude from his face anymore, and one eye was bulging from the socket.

I was suddenly able to move. I didn't know if that meant David was dead or just unconscious, and I didn't care. "Orson, come here!"

Orson trotted over to me. I wrapped my arms around him.

Madison continued screaming at David. "I loved you! You aren't going back to her!" It seemed David wasn't the only one to take rejection badly. David feebly tried to raise his arms in front of his face. She straddled him, raised the stone with both hands, and brought it down one final time. She let out a maniacal laugh. Her eyes were bloodshot, and an electric-blue halo crackled around her. "Now I'll show you how a powerful witch does things!"

Our problems with Yareth were over. But our problems with Madison were just beginning.

Orson whined. It felt odd not to hear him in my head.

"Come on," I told Orson. "We've got to move." I staggered to my feet and limped over to Wendy. I pushed the bench off of her. "Are you all right?"

"Ooh, not really."

"Can you move?"

"I think so. What happened?"

I helped her up. "Turns out Madison was running the show the whole time. She just killed her boyfriend in a jealous rage, and now she's mad at us."

"No shit?" She sounded both impressed and worried.

On cue, Madison shouted, "Where do you think you're going?"

I was fed up with her. "To get a stake to burn you on, psycho."

Madison screamed her displeasure. "I should have just killed you when you came to my apartment. Yareth didn't think I could handle you. He was wrong about that." She giggled. "He was wrong about a lot of things."

She waved her hands, and all the detritus she had been tossing around came flying toward me. Orson yipped and barked. Wendy waved her hands, and I saw a shimmer as she created a shield. That helped, but smaller pieces were getting through the magic wall. I knelt and tried to cover up Orson with my body as Wendy joined us.

"And you, you stupid, fat bitch," Madison called to Wendy. "You ran that coven into the ground. You shut it down rather than experience some real power and magic."

Debris was coming at us from all sides. Wendy couldn't hold it off for much longer. We scooted back but came up against the brick wall that surrounded the park. I tucked my chin to my chest. I could feel Orson's rapid breathing on my cheek.

"Enough!" Sheila shouted. "Madison, you've done enough damage."

"No, not hardly. But I have wasted enough time on this fat cow and your pathetic, useless boyfriend."

I glanced over my shoulder. Madison windmilled her arms. Blue light crackled around them. A second later, the park wall began to fall.

FORTY

THERE WAS A LOT OF screaming. Sheila screamed in horror. Madison screamed with laughter. Wendy screamed at me to get down. She put her hands up, shielding us from the worst of it with some kind of magical bubble. The bricks fell around us... mostly. I got knocked in the head by one. Blood trickled down my forehead and into my eye.

Madison yelled, "Now it's time to finish this! There's no room for weak, pretend witches who are too scared to use their power."

"Madison, do you know what you've done?" Sheila sounded angrier than I had ever heard her. There was steel in her voice, and even from across the plaza, I could see how dangerous her eyes were.

Orson squirmed. I loosened my hold on him and turned around in the rubble to see where Madison and Sheila were.

"Aside from eliminate all that was keeping—"

"Shut up! You've harmed the three things in this world that have kept me sane." Sheila pointed at Ramona. "My coven." She aimed her finger at Orson and me. "My familiar bond. My love."

Madison scoffed, "Those are all things that make you weak."

"Really?" Sheila's eyes glowed with a golden fire. She punched a fist into her open palm, and Madison rocked back on her heels. "You want to tell me how weak I am?"

Madison gasped. She waved her hands and sent debris flying at Sheila. Sheila didn't even flinch. Every piece either fell short or flew wide.

I crawled out of the brick pile then helped Wendy and Orson. A brick Sheila deflected zoomed past my head and into a part of the wall that was still standing. The barrier shuddered from the impact.

Wendy grabbed my arm. "Let's find better cover."

I nodded. We moved as fast as we could back to the Dead Sea Cave. Once we got there, I put Orson behind the wall then leaned around it to watch. I wanted to help Sheila, but I didn't think there was anything I could do. And if I went out there, I would probably just distract her.

"You stupid child!" Sheila said. "You thought Lisa and Wendy were *holding you back?* That they were trying to keep you down?" She punctuated each question with the barest flick of her finger.

Madison reacted to those flicks as if she were on the receiving end of multiple open-handed slaps. She screamed and waved her arm. A wave of energy radiated outward, and I even felt it from our hiding place. It knocked me back on my heels.

Sheila didn't even seem to notice. "Do you even begin to understand what you're dealing with? Lisa wasn't weak; she was strong. Do you know how strong you'd have to be *not* to unleash all of your power and destroy a parasite like David? Do you know how strong *I* had to be not to destroy the entire town I grew up in? They weren't holding you down; they were teaching you control." Sheila wasn't flicking her finger anymore. She was punching the air like a shadow boxer, blue sparks flying off with each blow. "You know what kept me from embracing all of the anger and rage and pain and just killing and hurting and destroying everything? My faith. My dog. My love. And you, stupid girl, have stepped on all three."

Madison was bleeding from her mouth and nose. Her eyes were glassy as she rocked on her feet.

"You have ruined all that is good for me. There is nothing in this world keeping me from destroying you."

Madison fell to the ground. She tried to shield herself with the stone, but Sheila snapped her fingers, and the gem flew to her. Madison was defenseless, broken and beaten.

I remembered what Sheila had told me: *The evil things we do leave a mark. Too many marks, and the soul is lost.* Madison was a horrible person. She had caused us pain and suffering. But that did not mean that we had the right to kill her.

I ran out of the cave and raced over to them, waving my arms. "Sheila, stop! If you kill her, you'll be no better than they are."

She looked over at me, and her eyes softened. But then she scowled. "No! She needs to feel what she's done. They tried to kill you. She isn't leaving here." She gave the air in front of her a devastating uppercut.

Madison flew about two feet of the ground then dropped and landed with a thud next to the unmoving corpse of David. Sheila cradled the stone in her left arm and advanced, fury set on her face.

Wendy caught up to me. "We need to stop this. She's stronger than anything I've ever seen. Her anger, her natural talent, and that stone are creating a perfect storm. If we don't do something, this whole park could be a crater."

"*What?*"

"You saw what Yareth did to my shop. He was an amateur, and Madison is a novice. Sheila is powerful. We have to talk her down."

"But... what could happen to her?"

Wendy shook her head. "I don't know. Maybe she's safe

at the eye of the storm, but more likely, all that rage will consume her completely."

Something nudged my foot. I looked down and saw Orson staring up at me with sad eyes.

Wendy nodded. "You heard her. Her faith, her love, her familiar. That's us. We can do it together."

"Wendy, can you still hear Orson? I can't." It felt so empty without him.

"Yes, but much more faintly."

I knelt in front of him. "Orson, we've got to help Mama. I'm sorry she released you, but she only did it to save me. She loves you."

Orson whined and tipped his head down to his paws.

Wendy said, "He understands. He says you owe him a taquito."

I smiled. "That's my boy. Let's go help her out."

We all stepped toward Sheila. The air was charged and crackling with power and rage.

I moved out in front, my hands in clear view. I didn't want to do anything to surprise her. "Sheila, you have to stop this."

Sheila was standing over a barely conscious Madison. She held the stone in both hands. "Don't try it, Gabriel. You have no right. I know how angry you've gotten. I know what you've done. You have no right to judge me."

"I'm not judging you. These assholes have put you through the wringer. I hope Madison gets everything coming to her, but we don't have to be the ones to do it."

Wendy came up to stand by my side. "That's right, dear. I know this isn't what you want. You're angry. You aren't thinking this through."

Sheila's eyes were pure gold tinged with purple as she glanced at Wendy. "What do you know about it?"

In a calm voice, Wendy answered, "I know you are someone who would rather hide out in an abandoned hotel than see those you love come to harm."

"They tried to take everything from me!" Sheila spoke through teeth clenched so hard I thought they might shatter.

"I know," Wendy said. "They tried to destroy my coven and my business as well."

"Then why are you stopping me?"

"Because they failed. They couldn't destroy my faith. And they couldn't destroy yours either." Wendy pointed at me. "Your dog and your man travelled a thousand miles to find you. David tried, but all he did was make their love for you stronger."

I took a few steps toward her but had to stop a few feet away. There was some kind of shield around her. "Sheila, I love you. I'm always going to love you. But you can't do this."

"No! No one tells me what I can or can't do. And you're wrong, Wendy. She didn't fail. Ramona betrayed me. And Orson is lost to me. Someone has to pay for that!"

"Sheila, you can't do this," I cried. "You taught me that. You told me what happens if you go down this path. Please, you have to remember!"

Sheila shook her head and raised the stone over Madison's head. The rock was shiny red in places with bits of David clinging to it. Then something jerked her back. She spun around, stone in hand, anger and confusion on her face.

Orson was behind her, biting on the hem of her dress and tugging it. He let go and sat down, staring up at her with the saddest eyes in the world. *Mama, I never released you.*

I could hear him again. And if I could hear him, his voice must have been a shout for Sheila.

Sheila dropped the stone and lowered her hands. The shield fell, and I stumbled forward. I ran over and wrapped my arms around her. When I touched her skin, I felt a shock as if I'd scuffed my feet on a carpet first. She started to cry as she sagged to the ground.

Orson licked her face. *Mama, I never let you go.*

A great cloud of tension lifted. Sheila began sobbing, and I cried on her shoulder.

Orson snuffled. *I still choose you.*

I glanced at Wendy. "How...?"

Wendy looked at Orson, who was slobbering all over us. "I told you he was stronger than any familiar I knew of. And you said he was stubborn. I guess he didn't want to be released."

Orson licked my face. *Nope. The pack stays together.*

Behind us, Madison rolled onto her side and spit on the ground. "Pathetic."

"Oh, shut up." Wendy shot some last jolt of magic.

Madison went down and didn't say anything else.

Sheila raised an eyebrow at Wendy. "Didn't you just say I shouldn't hurt her?"

Wendy shrugged. "I just said you shouldn't kill her. I didn't say we should let her walk out of here scot free. Besides, I didn't get a chance to hit David. Do you know what the estimates on my restaurant are?"

Sheila laughed. It was the best sound in the world.

FORTY-ONE

A FTER A FEW MORE MINUTES of the group hug, Sheila got up and went to check on her coven leader. Ramona was coming around, and hopefully, her own magic would leave her with just a nasty bruise and a headache.

That was more than David could hope for. He was extremely dead. Madison was out cold. Wendy was obviously skilled at both sandwich-making and knockout spells.

Rocks began moving in the pile of rubble. From underneath a toppled palm tree, a pale hand reached out, followed by a pale face and greasy, black hair.

I strolled over to little Malvolio as he tried to free himself from the debris. "Hello, Morty."

His eyes widened. His mouth formed a perfect O as he tried to scream, but no sound came out.

I walked over and held out a hand. "Quite a day, huh?"

He gingerly took my hand, and I pulled him to his feet. I felt kind of bad for him. He had been taken for a ride by Madison and David, and that was mainly due to the twin demons of teenage angst and teenage lust. We'd all been there.

Still, he did help kidnap Orson and hold Sheila captive. "What did you see before you got buried?" I asked.

"Well, um... I... um..."

"Did you see Madison break Yareth's skull open?"

He nodded meekly.

"And did you see Sheila wipe the floor with Madison?"
Another weak nod.

I grabbed the front of his shirt and pulled him close.
"Okay, so here's the deal. You're going to leave here. You're
going to tell the rest of your little playgroup that the magic
club is closed. Done. Gone forever. And then you're going
to go and help your mom clean up the mess you guys
made in her store. And you are never, ever going to play
with magic again. If I hear you so much as did a card trick
or pulled a quarter out of your cousin's ear or played 'got
your nose' with a baby, I will come back and feed you to
those gators one piece at a time. Got it?"

Morty was shaking, but he managed to say, "Yes. Got
it."

I let go of his shirt, giving him a little shove. "Good.
Now get out. You have one minute. And I never want to see
your sorry face again."

He ran toward the entrance. I'd never seen him move
so fast.

Sheila managed a weak smile. "You probably could
have just waved a wand at him. He would've been even
more scared."

I nodded. "True, but that was so much more satisfying."

She tried to laugh, but her heart wasn't in it yet. She
peered over at Madison's crumpled form and shuddered.
Then Sheila noticed the stone, which had rolled a few feet
away from her. Her eyes glistened with new tears. Quickly,
I scooped up the rock and held it out of her line of sight.

Wendy gestured at David and Madison. "I think we
need to figure out what to do with these... people."

A moan came from the far side of the plaza. It was the
security guard that David and Madison had knocked out
on their entrance.

"How strong do you think Madison is without the
stone?" I asked.

Wendy put a finger to her chin. "Without the stone

and without David and the rest of them? Hard to say. She wasn't that strong when we first met."

"Would she be able to break out of a prison? Just as one example."

"Probably not. She might be able to hypnotize a guard or two, but I don't think her magic would be enough to get all the way out of a real prison."

"Okay, I have an idea." I walked across the plaza and shook the shoulder of the moaning security guard. "Hey, wake up!"

"Huh? What...?"

"That was amazing! You're a hero!"

He looked around with a dazed expression. "What happened?"

I pointed at Madison and David. "These two satanists broke in here! They were going to set off a bomb in the park as part of some devil worship ritual. But you got here and surprised them. The girl panicked and set the bomb off early. It killed the guy and knocked you and her out. If you hadn't come by when you did, the damage would have been much worse."

"I don't remember any of that." He scratched his head while he surveyed the wreckage. "Really?" The area certainly looked as if a bomb had gone off, and I was pretty sure that Wendy and Sheila could make any security footage nothing but static.

Sheila came over and gazed into the guy's eyes. "Are you sure you don't remember? It seems clear to me that you stopped a great tragedy. I mean, you would be a hero."

The guard shook his head. "Of course, I remember! Yes, they were going to cause a lot of damage."

I raised my hands. "It's a miracle!"

Sheila rolled her eyes. "Yes, truly. You should thank God for the strength it took to stop those two."

The guard climbed to his feet. "I better get the police!"

Wendy said, "I think you should wait about thirty

minutes before you do that. Secure the scene first and make sure no one else is hiding out."

He touched his head. "Oh, right! What was I thinking?"

"And remember, you just found these two. No one else was here tonight."

"Well, of course!"

Wendy winked at him. "And if that satanic terrorist so much as looks at you cross-eyed, you whack her with your flashlight."

The guard nodded and walked over to Madison's prone body. Sheila and I hauled Ramona to her feet, put her arms around our shoulders, and dragged her out of the park. Wendy walked behind us, carrying the stone, and Orson trotted along beside us.

FORTY-TWO

WE DRAGGED RAMONA OUT TO the parking lot and sat her on the hood of my car. I took the stone from Wendy and put in the trunk, away from Ramona's greedy little hands.

When I returned, Ramona seemed more alert. "What happened?" she asked.

Sheila moved to stand in front of her. "Ramona, we're done. I can't believe what you had me do. I can't believe the situation you put me in. I want nothing more to do with you."

Ramona rubbed the bump on her head. "Don't be stupid. You need the coven. You think you can handle yourself against the next asshole who finds something magical? Maybe *that* guy's not a complete idiot. There's strength in numbers."

"Yes, but it also matters which numbers you choose. You're a negative. I don't need you."

Ramona puffed up as much as she could with her head still trying to lean to one side. "Fine. Give me the stone, and I'll be on my way."

Sheila gave a weary sigh. "I wouldn't give you that stone if you were the last witch on earth."

Ramona scowled. "What are you talking about?"

"I trust you about as much as I'd trust David with it. Less, in fact. He was a power-hungry douchebag, but at least he was honest about it."

"I am not leaving here without it." Ramona stared daggers at us. Her hands were loose and ready by her sides.

Orson growled. Wendy walked over to stand next to Sheila. I stayed a step behind the pair. I knew better than to get between a bunch of angry witches.

Wendy chuckled. "Oh, I think you are. Have a lovely flight back to New York. MCO is notorious for its long security lines, so you'd better get there early. Like *right now* early."

Ramona seethed, but one glance at the glowing eyes of Sheila, Wendy, and Orson, and she knew she was outgunned. "This isn't over. You have no right to that stone."

"I have as much right as you or anyone else does," Sheila responded calmly.

Ramona wagged a finger at her. "I hope you're happy. You've foregone your coven, your home, for a dog and some man."

Sheila shook her head. "You're wrong. It's the right man and the right dog. I could not be happier. Thank you for all you've taught me, but it's time I moved on."

Wendy checked her watch. "The hero guard is going to call the cops in twenty minutes, so it's time we moved on as well." She glanced dismissively at Ramona. "I wish I could say it was a pleasure to meet you, but it wasn't."

Ramona frowned, but she had no comeback. We piled into the car and drove off, leaving her standing in the parking lot.

We were a few miles down I-4, heading back to Wendy's shop, before I asked, "So what do we do with the stone?"

No one responded.

I cleared my throat. "Sheila, do you want to keep it?"

"No. I do not. It's very powerful, but you could see how hard it was to control that power. I almost lost myself." Her eyes misted.

"There were extenuating circumstances."

She laughed. "You've been watching *Law & Order*, using big words like that."

I chuckled. "Really, though. You'd lost your familiar. I was about to die. That would be stressful for anyone."

Sheila shook her head. "Believe me, I've had enough of that stone."

"So... what then? Do we go back to St. Augustine and bury it in the sand? What's to stop the next David or Madison from digging it up?"

Wendy leaned forward. "If I may, I might have a solution. Let's get to my store, and I'll show you."

———————————

I parked in front of Wendy's shop, and we all piled out of the car. I grabbed the stone out of the trunk. Wendy led us around to the back door. Once inside, she took us down to the basement.

"When Yareth and Madison were causing trouble the other night, they did more than just wreck my sign." She flicked on a light and pointed at the floor. "They managed to put a crack in the foundation."

The crack was about eight inches wide and went all the way through the concrete to the dirt underneath.

Wendy went over to a shelf against the far wall and returned with a folded tablecloth. "The contractors are coming tomorrow to fill it up. I think this would be a great place for the stone. What do you think?"

Sheila nodded. "This is perfect, Wendy."

Sheila didn't want to touch the gem, so I took the tablecloth and wrapped it around the stone. Lying on my belly, I stretched my arms down into the crack. I had to dig a little, but the split in the foundation had made the dirt pretty crumbly. I tucked the package into the hole I had made and covered it with dirt and some loose concrete pieces.

When I stood up, Wendy said, "Concrete should keep it in check. And I can protect it from misfits like Yareth." She looked at Sheila. "Besides, if you ever change your mind, you can always come back and get it."

I noticed that Orson still had the ring on his collar. I bent over and slipped it off. "Hey, you want to add this in as well?"

Wendy took the ring and gave it to Sheila. "Why don't you hang on to it? It might come in handy. If you practice with it, you'd be more likely to handle the big gem, if you ever needed it. It's a lot of power, but I'd trust it with the right person." She smiled. "And you've got a lot of right going for you."

Sheila hesitated before slipping the ring on her finger. Once it was in place, she shivered. "Even this is a lot to handle, but I think I can manage it. Just not right now." She took off the ring and put it in her pocket.

Wendy clapped her hands. "How about some coffee?"

We all agreed and headed upstairs to the restaurant. Wendy put on some coffee, and we sat at one of the tables to wait for it to brew.

Sheila leaned to the side and hugged Wendy. "Thank you so much. We couldn't have fixed this without you."

Wendy shook her head and pointed at me. "No. Thank Gabriel. He's the one who found me."

Sheila winked at me. "He'll get his thanks later."

No treats for me? Orson panted eagerly, giving Wendy his big, soft eyes.

Wendy laughed. "I think we can find something for you, provided Mama doesn't object."

Sheila bent over and gave Orson a pat. "I think he's earned a few hundred treats."

Really? Is that a promise?

Wendy got up and walked over to the meat counter. "Don't get your hopes up. I still have a business to run." She sliced some salami, put it on a plate, and set it down in front of Orson, who wolfed it down eagerly. "So what are you going to do now?" she asked Sheila.

Sheila shrugged. "I really hadn't considered it. I don't feel comfortable going back to New York. I don't trust the coven anymore, and I'm sure Ramona is going to spend her return flight writing an eviction notice for me." She glanced at me. "I'm sorry, Gabriel."

I put my arm around her. "I spent six years in the army living out of a duffle bag and getting bounced from base to base. It's no problem for me. Well, aside from the Mets games on TV." I grinned, and Sheila rolled her eyes. "Don't you need to get anything from the apartment?" I asked.

"I don't have that much stuff. And there's nothing there I care to go back for. I have a few sentimental items, but Lisa can get those for me. Besides, everything important is right here." She took my hand and scratched Orson's neck with her other one.

I gave her a quick kiss that ended up being a lot longer than I intended.

Wendy cleared her throat. "You know you're all welcome to stay here until you figure out what you want to do next."

Sheila shook her head. "Thank you, but we've already imposed too much. And I've been cooped up in a Florida hotel for too long, even if I wasn't awake for it. I need to get out and spread my wings." Sheila gave me a sultry gaze. "You feel like a road trip?"

"I can't wait. Just let me fix the radio first."

FORTY-THREE

T HREE DAYS LATER, ORSON WAS curled up next to Sheila on a blanket on Virginia Beach. She was scrunching her toes into the hot white sand and scratching Orson's neck when I returned from my walk.

"Here you go." I passed her an iced coffee. "That shop even makes the ice cubes out of coffee, so it won't get watered down." I sat down next to her.

"Thanks, sweetie." She kissed me on the cheek then took a sip. "Mmmm, it's perfect."

"I got a paper for us." I passed her a copy of the *Washington Post*. "Hey, check out page two. There's a story about that domestic terrorist cell in Orlando that tried to blow up Bible Land."

"You don't say!"

The "terrorist attack" had been national news. Satanists accused of blowing up a Christian tourist trap, but foiled by a righteous guard, was a juicy story and perfect for the dog days of summer. An anonymous tipster had led the police to the wreckage of Madison's trailer and her dead mother. That girl would be going away for a long time. Her lawyer would most likely try for an insanity defense, since she kept babbling about witches and magic stones. But none of the associates she named had any memory of her. Either Morty had gotten the rest of the group to shut up about her, or Wendy had done a few mind tricks.

Did you forget me? Orson gave me his sad eyes.

"I made you a promise, didn't I?" I reached into the 7-Eleven bag I had kept out of his sight and brought out some of its contents.

Taquitos!

I handed him one. "You earned them."

Sheila crinkled her nose. "How can you eat those things?"

Delicious!

She slapped my arm. "And how could you give them to him? You know how gassy they make him!"

"Hey, you say no to that face."

Orson looked up at her, his face covered with drool and what the taquito company claimed was beef.

Sheila laughed. "I guess you're right."

The sand was warm, and the sky was blue. The only sour note was the airplane. A stunt pilot was tooling around above the water. The loop-de-loops and death drops were amusing for about ten minutes, but then the noise got to be annoying. He had been at it since I had left to get the coffee twenty minutes ago.

"Orson?" When he looked up, I pointed at the plane.

With pleasure. He's making it hard to eat.

Orson stared up at the sky and barked. The plane stuttered, and the engine stalled. As the aircraft dipped toward the water, Orson barked again, and the engine roared back to life. The pilot steered the plane around and headed inland.

"Good boy! You let him land safely."

Orson panted happily. *I had to think about it.*

Sheila was aghast. "I can't believe you two! That pilot could have been hurt!"

Could have, should have. He's been buzzing around us for an hour.

"Honey, you can't tell me you were enjoying that racket."

She rolled her eyes. "No, but I would have enjoyed him crashing into the ocean less!"

Orson gave her the sad eyes. *I'm sorry, Mama. Gabriel made me.*

I spoke up. "I'm sorry, but I needed some quiet." I fumbled around in my pocket and took out another bag.

"You don't get to boss Orson around, especially now that I'm back."

"I know." My hands had suddenly gotten very sweaty. "Sheila, I've always loved you. And these last few weeks, I realized how much I need you and how much I need to let you know that." I passed her the bag.

On the way to get coffee, I had found a street vendor selling handmade jewelry. The pewter ring wasn't expensive, but it would have to do. Two dolphins on the front framed the shape of a heart.

She fished the ring out of the bag. "Oh, Gabriel."

"I know it's not Tiffany's, but seeing as we are homeless and all..."

She threw her arms around my neck. "Shut up! It's perfect. Yes!"

"I didn't even get to ask you yet."

So hurry up, Dad.

"Will you marry me?"

"Even though you're homeless? Of course!" Her eyes were wet with tears, and she beamed as she pulled me in for a kiss.

We sat on that beach for a long time. Sheila leaned against me, resting her head on my shoulder as we gazed out at the water. Orson curled up at our feet to doze after his feast of taquitos. There were a lot of beaches, and I was thinking we could see them all if we tried.

ABOUT THE AUTHOR

 Victor Catano lives in New York City with his wonderful wife, Kim. When not writing, he works in live theater as a stage manager, light designer, and technical director, working mainly with dance companies. His hobbies include coffee, Broadway musicals, and complaining about the NY Mets and Philadelphia Eagles.